Flash Point

Flash Point

Sneed B. Collard III

PEACHTREE PUBLISHERS
1700 Chattahoochee Avenue
Atlanta, Georgia 30318-2112

www.peachtree-online.com

Cover design by Loraine M. Joyner
Book design by Melanie McMahon Ives

Jacket front cover photograph: Extreme fire behavior on the Blackhall Fire
Encampment, Wyoming, 2000.

Manufactured in United States of America

10 9 8 7 6 5 4 3 2 1
First Edition

Library of Congress Cataloging-in-Publication Data

Collard, Sneed B.
  Flash point / by Sneed B. Collard, III. -- 1st ed.
    p. cm.
  Summary: After school Luther works part-time with a vet who
rescues and retrains birds of prey but when he questions many of
the community's beliefs about land use, he risks alienation from
his friends and family.
  ISBN 1-56145-385-4
  [1. Ecology--Fiction. 2. Nature--Fiction. 3. Birds of prey
--Fiction. 4. Montana--Fiction.]   I. Title.
PZ7.C67749Fla 2006
[Fic]--dc22
                                        2006013997

To the memory of Pam Tabish,
a dedicated librarian and friend,
who flew from us far too soon.

—S. B. C. III

One

As soon as he burst through the large double doors, the smoke hit him like a diesel locomotive. The acid pall stung his eyes and burned his throat. Ashes swirled around him and overhead the September sun glowered red like one of those dissolving tablets used to color Easter eggs. Luther Wright pulled a handkerchief out of his pocket and held it over his nose.

"Whew," he said. "It's even worse than yesterday."

His friend Chet coughed. "Yeah. The winds must be blowing from the north."

All around them, students spilled like whitewater down the front steps of Heartwood High School, eager to put distance between themselves and the school day. Almost all of them, though, paused to look up at the eerie orange-black clouds overhead. Their faces showed that even in Heartwood, fires like this were a major event.

The flames had been burning since the beginning of August. Ignited by Montana's driest summer in more than a decade, dozens of fires had erupted throughout the western half of the state. The Rocky Gulch blaze, fifteen miles north of Heartwood, had by itself charred 120,000 acres—an area larger than the sprawling city of Denver, Colorado. The inferno had been burning more than three weeks and Luther could barely remember the last time he'd seen blue sky. Today seemed the worst yet.

"Well, at least they cancelled afternoon football practice," Chet said as he and Luther walked toward the bike racks. "Me and some of the other guys thought we'd go down to Sky Burger and hang out. You want to come?"

Luther was tempted. The year before, he'd also been on the football team—a solid freshman linebacker and, with his high-intensity play, a shoo-in to make varsity. But to everyone's shock, he'd decided not to go out this year. Already he could feel a distance growing between him, Chet, and the other players.

"Ah, I'd better not," Luther mumbled, reluctant to disappoint his friend. "I've got to get out to Kay's to take care of the birds."

Suddenly, a brawny Neanderthal with a crimson crew cut bulldozed his way through to them. "You and those friggin' birds!" the hulk said. "What kind of idiot takes care of pests anyway?"

Luther's jaw set. Warren Juddson was about the last person he wanted to have a conversation with. Warren was the third of seven kids in the Juddson clan, and, like the rest of his family, trouble followed him like smoke. His oldest brother Jack had landed in the state penitentiary at Deer Lodge for assault with a deadly. The second oldest,

Raymond, had somehow kept a job at the mill with their father, Knot Juddson—when the mill wasn't shut down or Ray wasn't sleeping it off in County.

Warren did his best to follow the family tradition. He'd already been suspended for fighting once this year, and rumor had it he was failing every class but metal shop and phys ed. Everyone knew that if it weren't for Warren's bulk and ferocity as a defensive tackle, the school would have booted him long ago.

Before this year, Luther hadn't had any particular problem with Warren. Since Luther had decided not to go out for football, however, Warren had been getting in his face on a regular basis. Luther was sick of it.

"Hawks and eagles aren't pests," he told Warren. "They're predators. They eat pests like mice and rats—and Juddsons."

"I don't care what you call 'em," Warren said, stepping closer. "I call 'em target practice."

A couple of other football players laughed, and Luther knew he couldn't just let this one slide. He straightened up and looked Warren in the eyes. Warren had thirty pounds on him, but Luther moved faster. Besides being on the football team, he had also gone out for wrestling the year before. If it came to blows, Luther figured Warren could probably take him, but then again, he might not. He stared down the bigger boy until he saw the flicker of doubt in his eyes.

Warren stepped back and raised an imaginary gun to his shoulder. "Just don't bring one of those birds in range of my 12-gauge—or *boom!*"

"Give it a rest, Warren," Chet said.

Warren and Luther glared at each other for another second. Then Warren grinned.

"Aw, I'm just jerkin' you around," he said, his smile exposing two gaping holes where teeth should have been.

"Well, go jerk somewhere else," Luther said, feeling the adrenaline pump through him.

"It'll be a relief, birdbrain," Warren said, shoving off with four others from the football team.

"Douche-bag," Chet muttered.

"Yeah," said Luther. "Does that moron ever think before he opens his mouth? If I had to choose between Warren and a raptor, I'd pick a bird any day. Raptors at least serve some purpose in the world."

"Maybe you know that and I know it, but don't forget you're in Heartwood, Montana," Chet said. "Some people around here, if they see a hawk or eagle or falcon, are going to shoot first and ask questions later. Admit it, Luth. Before you met Kay, you didn't know a thing about raptors, let alone care about them."

"That's not true."

Chet looked at him, eyebrow cocked.

"Well...maybe a little true," Luther conceded.

"Besides, Warren's just trying to rub your face in it because you're not on the team anymore. It makes him feel superior."

"I know." But Luther also knew there was more to the bad blood between him and Warren than Chet or anyone else understood. He bent down and began dialing the combination on his bike lock.

"Hey, Luth?"

He straightened back up. "Yeah?"

"Uh, any chance you'll join the wrestling team again? I know you said you didn't want to, but I talked to Coach and it's not too late. We could really use you in the 152-pound division. If you started training now, you'd be ready for the first meet."

Especially after quitting football, Luther had often thought about going out for wrestling again. Most of his friends from the football team were also wrestlers. But the incident at the end of last year's football season had pretty much killed his interest in sports—any sports.

"Thanks, Chet, but—"

Suddenly, Luther's eyes focused on a girl in jeans and a turquoise shirt walking down the school's front steps.

He nudged his friend. "Hey, Chet, do you know that girl?"

Chet followed Luther's gaze. The girl carried a green backpack and wore her reddish brown hair tied back in a ponytail. Luther had seen her once before, but didn't know her name—a small miracle in Heartwood, where you couldn't empty the trash without a full account of it showing up in the local newspaper.

"Oh, her," Chet said. "Her name's Alexandra or Amanda or something like that. She just moved here from Billings. Her dad's the new Fish and Wildlife warden. Why?"

Luther shrugged. "Just curious. Anyway, I'd better get going."

Chet nodded. "See you tomorrow."

"Yeah, see you then."

Luther tied his handkerchief bandit-style around his nose and mouth, mounted his rusting ten-speed, and pedaled east on the old highway, away from school. Technically, with a Stage 2 Air Alert, you weren't supposed to even be outside, but no one let that stop them around here. In Montana, people did what they had to, forest fires or not.

As Luther rode, half a dozen cars and pickup trucks passed him, mostly filled with seniors whooping and celebrating the cancellation of after-school sports practices. Luther knew that most of them were headed to Ambush Point to drink beer. He did his best to ignore them. After about a mile, he turned right, at a sign marked "Elk Flats Road." He bounced across the Montana Rail Link tracks and arrived home a few minutes later.

Luther's mom called their white and green house a "work-in-progress." His mom and stepfather Vic bought it when they moved to Heartwood twelve years ago. It had only one bedroom then, but every time they'd scraped together a little money, his stepdad added on a room or pantry or something. Luther figured that in another twenty years, there'd be so many rooms and passageways, they could call it the Heartwood House of Mystery and sell tickets to tourists off the interstate.

A '96 red Neon sat next to the house when he rolled to a stop. Even before his feet touched ground, his Border collie Roadkill barked and came racing toward him from the field next door. Luther leaned his bike against the garage and stumbled as the dog wriggled against his legs.

Luther crouched and pulled the handkerchief down to his neck. "How are you, crazy dog?"

Roadkill licked both sides of Luther's face and submitted to being petted for exactly five seconds. Then he jumped back and stared, full of expectation.

Luther laughed. "We'll go in a minute. I've got to put my stuff down and change."

Roadkill followed Luther into the house, where they found his stepsister Brenda and her girlfriend, Samantha, or "Sam," the owner of the red Neon out front.

"There he is," Brenda teased. "Heartwood's original rebel."

"Hey, Luther," Sam called. "What's happening?"

Brenda and Sam were both seniors and two of the most popular girls at Heartwood High. Besides banking some serious good looks, Brenda had made varsity cheerleader for the past two years and Sam headed the drill team. The two were sprawled on opposite ends of the living room couch, each holding a can of beer, while Oprah blared from the idiot set.

Luther shifted his backpack from one shoulder to the other. "Vic's going to kill you if he finds out you're drinking his beer."

"He won't," Brenda said. "If he ever gets home from fighting fires, he'll be too tired to notice anything. Besides, we'll get him a new six-pack."

"Come pop a can with us, Luth," Sam said.

"No thanks."

"What's the matter? Last year, you were a party animal. You too good for us now?"

"I've just got other things to do."

Brenda shook her head at Sam. "I try to bring him up right, but it's no use."

Luther couldn't help cracking a smile as he led Roadkill to his room. Brenda tried to be a good big sister. When Luther was younger, he'd idolized Brenda as the coolest person on earth with her hip, beer-drinking friends and endless parties. He'd always felt proud when she invited him to do things or introduced him to her friends at school. When Luther had become a freshman a year ago, he'd launched full-throttle into the partying scene himself.

Not this year. Now it felt like he and Brenda—he and *everyone*—were orbiting different planets.

Luther flung his pack on his bed, then changed into his work clothes—old jeans and a plaid shirt, each stained with bird poop, and a pair of hand-me-down work boots that should have been in a museum. He went in the kitchen, fixed himself a bowl of cereal, and took it to the living room, where he plopped down in his stepdad's ratty recliner.

Sam set her beer can on the coffee table. "Going to see the birds again?"

Luther nodded and shoved a spoonful of Wheat-Os into his mouth.

"Those birds have gone to his head," Brenda told Sam. "He's decided he likes them better than people."

"Is that true?" Sam asked. "Do you like birds better than people?"

Luther took another bite. *"Some* people," he said, shooting his sister a smart-assed look. "Some times."

"Ooh!" Sam said, bursting into laughter.

"You better watch it, little brother," Brenda taunted. "You're still not too old for me to take you across my knee!"

"That sounds fun," said Sam. "Can I help?"

"Naw, he's wearing his smelly bird clothes. Besides, Luther isn't interested in girls," Brenda said.

Sam's face suddenly grew conspiratorial. "Luther, you're not in the closet, are you?"

Brenda almost choked on her beer, and Luther's face turned cherry red. "No," he stammered.

"So what's wrong with girls, then?" Sam asked.

How could he explain it? He liked girls plenty. They just didn't seem to like *him*—at least not the ones he was interested in. Luther didn't consider himself bad-looking. He had a decent build, and his dark hair and deep-set eyes gave him a sort of gawky Johnny Depp look. It was just that he didn't stand out. Even when he'd been on the football team, he never seemed to draw a glance from the really good-looking girls. And he never could think of much to say to the more interesting ones—the brainy girls or those with some personality.

"It doesn't matter," he told Sam, getting up from the recliner. He walked his cereal bowl in to the kitchen and then headed toward the front door. "Come on, Roadkill. Let's get to work."

Two

uther veered right out of his driveway and again pedaled east on Elk Flats Road. Roadkill cantered easily alongside, his tongue flapping joyfully with every step. The road turned to dirt after a hundred yards, and they crossed over a bridge made from an old flatbed railcar. Cottonwoods towered above them, creating a shady tunnel. With every crank of his pedals, Luther could feel himself grow lighter and happier—something that used to happen to him heading out onto the football field. Now, coming to Kay's did it.

He'd first met Kay the previous June. Luther, like everyone else in Heartwood, had known about her since she'd come up from Louisiana a couple of years before, answering a general ad for a large animal vet. She bought the old Russell farm outside of town and set up practice. At first people gossiped about her. Some Heartwood residents didn't know what to think of a woman living all alone, doctoring cows, horses, and pigs, but Kay quickly proved herself. After a year of seeing her assisting births, curing diseases, treating colic, and performing other life-saving miracles, most folks began going out of their way to help her and pay her respect in the community.

Still, Luther had never met Kay before Roadkill tangled with a porcupine the day after school let out. The quills punctured Roadkill's flesh like nails. Luther had pulled out as many as possible, but he didn't dare touch the ones in the dog's ears and mouth. Luther rushed Roadkill out to Kay, who patiently tracked down each quill and clipped the ends so that they'd collapse and be easier to pull. As she yanked them out, Kay talked soothingly to the Border collie, and, amazingly, Roadkill hadn't struggled or whimpered, even when the vet extracted quills from the tender flesh of his left ear.

After Kay finished, Luther asked about the fee. "I don't have any money right now," he told her.

Kay looked at him thoughtfully and asked, "You need a job?"

While Roadkill licked his wounds on Kay's living room couch, the vet took Luther out to see her birds. She showed him the golden eagle, the great-horned owl, the kestrels, and the others. She even perched a prairie falcon on his hand. After half an hour, Luther was hooked. Since that time, he'd been coming out here six or seven days a week—even when Kay didn't need him.

Today, as Luther rattled down the dirt road, Kay's ramshackle collection of sheds and barns materialized one by one through the smoke. The farm sat on some of the prettiest land in Heartwood. Behind the buildings, the Clark

Fork River sparkled as it took a wide, meandering bend west. Cottonwoods and willows lined the bank. Beyond that, steep larch- and pine-covered mountainsides rose into the smoky gloom. Luther parked his bike under the ponderosa pine next to the main house and took a smoke-filled breath. He stretched his back muscles, feeling the vertebrae pop one by one.

Godzilla—Kay's big green '64 International Travelall—was missing from the driveway, but it wasn't unusual for her to be away on a call when Luther arrived. Now that the fires were coming closer, people called Kay out every day to look at animals affected by the smoke, heat, and flames. Luther didn't mind. Just being out here made him feel at peace like nothing else did. Roadkill at his side, he circled around the house to the small back porch that tripled as a work area and toolshed. Luther spotted Kay's old beat-up chainsaw hanging on the wall.

"I've got to lube and sharpen that thing for her," he reminded himself for the hundredth time, but right now he had other duties.

Next to the work sink, he found what he'd come back there for, a small plastic box full of thawed white mice. Kay got them from a genetics research lab over in Missoula. Once the lab techs had drawn blood from the mice, they needed to dispose of them, so they gave them to Kay—more than a hundred pounds of mouth-watering rodents every month. Kay kept them in two big freezers in one of the sheds, but every morning she removed a couple of dozen to thaw for the afternoon feeding.

Luther picked up the box, a large rawhide glove, and a bag containing two thawed rabbits—also donated to Kay by a local business.

"C'mon, Roadkill," he said, heading to the closest shed. Luther opened the door and the Border collie followed him inside. The acrid smell of guano, or bird poop, stung Luther's nostrils and he paused, waiting for his vision to adjust to the dim light. Kay had carved out two main partitions inside the shed, each separated by chicken wire. When Luther looked into the left partition, two huge golden eyes appeared, staring back at him.

"Stay," Luther told Roadkill. The dog sat and watched, his ears raised to full attention.

"How you doin', Elroy?" Luther asked. He unlatched the door of the cage and slowly approached the great horned owl. The owl bobbed its head up and down, never taking its eyes off Luther.

Luther felt a special affection for Elroy because he was the first bird he'd seen Kay work her magic on. A week or so after Luther started working there, a bicyclist found the owl starving in a field with a busted wing. Over the next few weeks, Luther watched Kay go through the slow process of trying to restore the bird to health. The wing had a clean break, away from the joints—probably the result of a collision with a tree—so Kay had been able to set it. She'd held off feeding Elroy right away.

"If you feed a starving bird right off," she'd explained to Luther, "they'll use their last energy to digest the food and it will kill them."

Instead, Kay had given Elroy a liquid mixture of electrolytes and a formula called Nutri-cal and placed him in a dark box with a heating pad.

"Why do you put him in a box?" Luther had asked.

"At first, you want to keep the birds' stress to a minimum," Kay had explained. "If you keep them dark, quiet, and still, that lets them rest. Just putting them in a box with a heating pad probably saves more birds than anything else I do."

Kay's efforts with Elroy had paid off. He'd bulked up to full weight, his wing had healed, and Kay hoped to release him back into the wild before winter arrived.

Luther opened the box of mice, and Elroy began shuffling back and forth on his perch.

"Yeah, you know what these are, don't you?" Luther said in a low voice. He picked up a dead mouse and held it out to the owl. The bird inhaled the mouse in one fast movement, so that only the rodent's tail hung from his beak. With another gulp, the tail also disappeared. Luther picked up a second mouse and gave it to Elroy. Then a third, for dessert.

"You're a hungry boy today, aren't you?"

Elroy again bobbed his head up and down, as if to nod, but Kay had told Luther that was the way owls judged distance.

"By seeing something from two different angles," Kay had explained, "they get better depth perception. It's called *parallax*. That's why they're always bobbing their heads up and down."

Luther put the lid back on the box of mice.

"See you later," he told Elroy, stepping out of the cage and latching it behind him. Next, he entered the adjacent partition, home to a small burrowing owl named Gopher. Gopher was a female, but only about a quarter the size of Elroy. Like Elroy, she'd come in with a broken wing, but not from an accident. Gopher had been shot and left for dead in the field behind Heartwood High School. Kay tried to save the wing, but ended up amputating it just above the elbow.

"Normally, since she'll never fly, I'd euthanize a bird like this," Kay had told Luther. "But I got attached to her and decided to keep her around." That happened a lot at Kay's. More than half her birds had permanent injuries—some from gunshots, others from getting caught in traps and fences. A few had been injured by accidentally slamming into power lines or windshields. Kay quickly put most of these damaged birds out of their misery, but others became part of her family. She took them around to local schools to teach kids about birds of prey and her work with them.

After giving Gopher a mouse, Luther led Roadkill to the shack Kay had named "Hawk Heaven." Inside, he fed two red-tails, a goshawk, and his favorite—a Cooper's hawk Kay had named "Alice" after one of her favorite rock stars. Unlike the owls, the hawks held down the mice with their talons while tearing them apart with their hooked beaks. As gory as it was, Luther was always fascinated by their dexterity and how efficiently they used the tools they were born with.

Leaving Hawk Heaven, Luther walked to two large open enclosures closer to Kay's house. In the first pen, Luther threw a rabbit to Groucho—a bald eagle that had been found tangled in some fishing line. Kay planned to release him as soon as he gained another pound or two. After closing Groucho's gate, Luther stepped into the second enclosure.

"Hey, Maxie," Luther called. Max, the golden eagle, stared at Luther from the ground near his open shelter. Like the burrowing owl, he was a permanent resident at Kay's.

"I think he got into some poison," Kay had told Luther. "Someone probably put it out for coyotes or something, and it messed up Max's head. He's not nearly as bold as a golden should be and will probably never be quite right."

Luther loved Max's gentle disposition. As Luther approached, he talked gently to the eagle, and Max didn't move or fidget. After a minute, Luther pulled out a rabbit and threw it to the bird.

"Bon appétit," he told Max as he left the pen.

Luther always saved his favorite stop for last—the falcon house. Though he admired all raptors—or birds of prey—the falcons flew closest to his heart. Not only were they the fastest of all raptors, Luther thought they were the most beautiful.

At the moment Kay had four of them: a prairie falcon, a peregrine, a kestrel, and the largest of all falcons, a gyrfalcon named Sal. The other three falcons had permanent injuries, but Kay had nursed Sal back to health from a

16

broken wing and decided to keep her to train and fly. After feeding the other three, Luther put on the heavy rawhide glove and entered Sal's cage.

"What a good bird," Luther crooned, stepping close to the small platform that served as a perch.

Sal blinked, but stayed calm. It had taken the gyr several weeks to get used to Luther, but now she accepted him as part of her routine.

Sal stood about sixteen inches high and weighed almost three pounds. She never failed to send shivers down Luther's spine. The gyr had recently completed her annual molt, and her new silver-white feathers shimmered like a royal cloak. Before feeding her, Luther placed his gloved hand at the base of her chest, right next to her feet. As she stepped onto his hand, Luther could feel the strength of her talons. If it weren't for the glove, Sal's claws could have squeezed through his flesh like butter. With his free hand, Luther stroked Sal's chest and ran his fingers cautiously over her wings. The silky smoothness and softness of her feathers always surprised and thrilled him.

"You're looking great today," he told Sal. He was reaching for a mouse when he heard Godzilla roar up the drive.

Three

L uther placed Sal back on her perch and walked toward Kay's '64 International, where his boss was unloading a flat of eggs and two gallons of milk. Kay wore her uniform of jeans, plaid shirt, and hiking boots. As usual, her blonde hair stuck out wildly in all directions, defying her minimal attempts to tame it.

Roadkill rushed ahead to greet her, and Kay set her load of food down to give him a vigorous head rub. "Hey Luth!" she called. "How's my favorite face?"

He smiled as he approached. "Pretty good."

"Glad to hear one of us is. What a day!"

"Where'd you get the eggs and milk?"

"Ah, I stopped by the Norgaards' place. I've been checking on one of their quarter horses with foot problems, and they always send me home with extra goodies. I think people around here worry I might starve to death without a good man to watch over me."

Luther laughed as he picked up the food. "They don't know you very well."

"You got that right. Besides, I got the best help a person could ask for right here."

The compliment brought an awkward grin to Luther's face.

Kay pulled a closed cardboard box from the truck and headed toward the back of the house. Luther and Roadkill followed her.

"Anyway," Kay said as they reached the back porch, "their horse was the least of it today. This fire stuff's freaking everybody out. The animals deal with it okay, but I'm getting calls from people worrying about smoke inhalation, burnt hooves, skin rashes, you name it. Most of it's harmless, but it makes people feel better to have me take a look."

"What's in the box?" Luther asked, setting the eggs and milk on a workbench.

"Oh." Kay placed the container on the ground next to the porch and sighed. "This is ugly."

She opened the cardboard flaps to reveal a large bird with a brown head and beautiful russet tail feathers. Luther stepped closer and the bird stared weakly up at him.

"A red-tail," he said.

"Yeah. For a male, it's a big one," Kay said. "But look at that wing."

A weight landed in Luther's stomach. The bird's left wing lay twisted into a mass of broken feathers and dried blood. The sharp, jagged end of a hollow wing bone poked out through the flesh.

"Where'd you get him?"

"One of the Montana Power people intercepted me just up the road. He found it while checking some high-voltage wires. I just thanked him and took the box."

"There's nothing you can do, is there?"

Kay shook her head. "Nope. I would have put this guy out of his misery right there, but it's bad PR to do it in front of other people. Whoever shot this bird had pretty good aim. Looks like there's at least half a dozen shotgun pellets in his breast."

Luther shifted so he could see the bird's breast feathers, and sure enough, they were speckled with dried blood.

"You want to handle this?" Kay asked.

Luther knew that technically he wasn't even supposed to touch one of these birds. Without a license, touching, interfering with, harming, or otherwise harassing any bird of prey was both a federal and state offense, punishable by fines and jail time. But Kay owned all the proper permits to work with raptors and also had an understanding with local officials. They knew Kay kept the birds' welfare first in mind, and as long as she used common sense, nobody messed with her. Still, Luther wasn't eager to help with this particular job.

"I'd rather not," he told Kay.

"I don't blame you. The worst part of working with these animals is when you can't save them."

Kay entered her house and emerged a moment later holding a needle and syringe. Luther knew from past experiences that the syringe contained a deadly dose of barbiturate.

As Kay crouched down next to the box, Roadkill crept forward, catching the scent of the bird.

"Back," Luther told the dog. The Border collie retreated a few steps, but kept staring intently.

Luther knelt next to Kay and looked at the hawk. The bird seemed to be sinking into shock. Luther cautiously ran his hand along its good wing. He tried to say something, but the words stuck in his throat and his vision blurred. He stood and took a step back to give Kay room.

His boss gently felt around for the brachial artery in the red-tail's good wing. Then, she slipped the needle in and emptied the syringe. "I'm sorry, buddy."

Luther took a deep breath. Even though he had seen this several times before, a wave of sadness overwhelmed him.

"God, I never get used to that," Kay said, straightening up. Luther saw her wipe the back of her hand across her cheek.

They stood quietly for a moment. "It seems like we've had a lot of these lately," Luther said.

"Yep. Something's going on. I've been asking around, but nobody's seen anything. Either that, or they're not telling."

They stood looking down at the dead hawk for another moment, and anger began to force the sadness from Luther's heart.

"How could people do this? These birds don't hurt anyone."

"I ask myself that every day, Luther. I guess a lot of it's

just prejudice that's been handed down from one generation to the next. Most people have come to realize that raptors are our friends. But there are still a few farmers, ranchers, and others who've learned to believe that predators—all predators—are their enemies."

"But why?"

Kay thought for a moment. "I think it comes from somewhere primitive inside of us. It's not so much that people fear being harmed by predators directly. It's that we're out there hunting just like they are. Some predators kill wild game that we'd like to eat. A few predators prey on the cows or the sheep we raise. That's why we've made up stories about how evil predators are and spent decades killing off wolves, coyotes, mountain lions, eagles—any animals that go after the same food we do. They're our competition."

"But we don't really compete with raptors."

"I'm not saying it makes sense," Kay told him. "I'm just saying that some fears go so deep that it's hard to get past them. Plus, there are always going to be a few idiots who just shoot at anything that flies. Anyway, do me a favor, Luth. I'm going to get rid of this needle. Would you mind double-bagging this guy and putting him in the freezer? I'm saving the carcasses, just in case they happen to nail someone for these shootings."

"Yeah, sure. C'mon, Roadkill."

Luther carried the box to the shed with the two large freezers. He gently slipped the red-tail into two plastic freezer bags and placed it in its frozen tomb. Then he and Roadkill joined Kay back at the house.

"I didn't feed Sal yet," Luther told Kay, walking through the back door.

Kay smiled. "I figured you might not have. What do you say we get our minds off the hawk and do a little flying?"

Luther didn't have to answer. Kay knew that after only three months, he loved to fly as much as she did. "I've got a couple of quail in the fridge," she said.

While Luther retrieved the quail, Kay put on her over-sized army surplus jacket and grabbed the case that held the transmitters they used in case Sal decided to make a break for it. Then they set off toward the pigeon coop. In addition to building the raptor houses, Kay had constructed a loft for the homing pigeons she used to train Sal. The pigeons were free to come and go as they pleased but were extremely docile. Kay stuffed four of them into the army jacket's huge pockets. Fully loaded, she and Luther walked to the falcon house.

"You know what to do," Kay said.

Luther hesitated. He'd never done this all on his own before.

"Sal will let you know if you do something wrong," Kay assured him.

"That eases my mind," Luther replied, with a layer of sarcasm. He'd seen the scars on Kay's hands where she'd been bitten and clawed by other raptors.

"Don't worry," said Kay. "I doubt that Sal would even like how you taste with all that high school junk food you eat."

"Very funny."

Luther unzipped the case that carried the two transmitters, small electronic devices with eight-inch single-wire antennae attached to them. Transmitters had become standard equipment for falconers—insurance for the rare cases when a bird decided to take off or met with an unfortunate accident while flying. Each transmitter emitted a different radio frequency, one offering backup in case the other failed. Lost birds could be tracked using a handheld antenna and a receiver dialed to each frequency.

"Easy does it," Luther said, approaching Sal. Using black plastic cable ties, he attached the transmitters to Sal's jesses—the leather straps dangling from her legs. Luther's fingers shook slightly as he snugged them down, but the bird just stared at him, used to the procedure.

"Perfect," Kay told him.

After he finished, Luther pulled on the thick leather glove and picked up a small leather hood.

"Come on, sweetie," he crooned to Sal.

"Sweetie?" Kay chuckled. "Luther, we need to get you a girlfriend—fast!"

Luther placed his gloved hand under Sal's chest and she stepped up obligingly. Next, he grasped Sal's jesses between his gloved thumb and forefinger to make sure she couldn't fly away.

"That's a good girl," he told her, lightly stroking her wings and chest. "Does she look okay?"

"You're doing fine," Kay said. "Just move nice and smooth."

Taking the leather hood in his left hand, Luther oriented it correctly and quickly slipped it over Sal's head. The hood completely covered the bird's eyes, but left her beak and breathing holes clear. The hood, Kay had explained, helped keep the birds calm. Raptors were so excitable that almost any sudden movement or noise could send them flapping around, breaking wing and tail feathers. Luther lightly tightened the hood's two draw straps, holding one in his free hand and the other in his teeth. To his relief, Sal didn't resist.

"Smooth as Ex-Lax," Kay said. "Let's go."

Following his boss, Luther left the shed, and together they walked to a large field beyond the sheds. Roadkill trotted alongside, his nose high, processing every whiff of Sal he could get. He kept a good distance away, though, and didn't jump or do anything else to upset the falcon.

"Good boy," Luther told him. "You know this is serious work, don't you?"

"Of course he does," said Kay, slipping the dog a treat as she walked.

By the time they reached the center of the field, the smoke from the Rocky Gulch fire had lightened.

"Looks like we're catching a break," Kay observed. "Maybe the wind's shifted."

"Yeah," Luther said, keeping his eyes on Sal.

"Okay, take off her hood and we'll see what she can do."

Luther loosened the straps and gently tugged the hood from Sal's head. Sal blinked and looked around, alert to every sound and movement. Roadkill crouched in the grass and waited for what came next.

"Let her rip," Kay said.

Luther released the leather jesses and made a quick upward movement with his arm. Sal leaped from his wrist and sped across the field. Roadkill jumped to his feet and watched. Sal flew two wide arcs around them and then landed on the bare branch of a snag, a dead cottonwood tree next to the river.

"She looks good," said Luther.

"Yeah. She's almost back to full strength after the accident and her molt. Let's see what she does with a pigeon."

Kay pulled one of the pigeons from her right pocket and threw it into the air. The pigeon darted across the field. Sal hunched over and watched it but remained perched on the snag.

"Spoiled bird," Kay muttered. "Here. You try."

She handed Luther a pigeon and Luther tossed it straight up. This time, Sal shot after it. The gyrfalcon's wings looked like a fighter plane's as she dove toward the pigeon and banked sharply right and then left. The pigeon countered by shooting higher and taking radical turns of its own.

Luther felt his heart race. This beats football and wrestling put together, he thought.

Sal chased the pigeon through five or six turns, nearly catching it twice. Then, she returned to her perch on the dead tree while the second pigeon joined the first one circling above their coop.

"That's my girl!" Kay shouted.

"Wow," said Luther. "She's almost there, isn't she?"

"Almost. Another week and maybe we can take her out hunting."

Early on, Kay had explained to Luther that hunting was the main activity of most falconers. What they hunted depended on what kind of birds they had. Peregrine falcons mostly hunted other flying birds, but a large gyr like Sal could nail rabbits, pheasants, and almost any other small animal. In a book from the school library, Luther had read that falconry actually began as a way for people to catch food for themselves. The book said that the practice probably started in China about 4,000 years ago and later spread to the Middle East and Europe. It peaked during the feudal times of the Middle Ages, when certain social classes could fly only certain kinds of birds.

Now any kind of bird could be flown by any person who was old enough and had gone through the right procedures, training, and certifications. Already, Luther knew that that's what he wanted to do—fly a bird of his own.

They released another pigeon into the air, and as they watched Sal swoop after it, Kay seemed to read Luther's mind.

"As soon as the right bird comes in—one we can patch up—we'll get you started training it."

Luther couldn't keep the smile from his lips. He and Kay had talked about this many times before. Kay had explained that most people began their falconing apprenticeship by catching a young wild bird, training it, and keeping it. But she had suggested that Luther start by training a young bird that had been injured and then releasing it back into the wild. Young birds often had poor hunting skills and most of them died their first year. By training one, Luther would not only learn about falconry, but would also increase the bird's chances of survival once it was released. The question was when and what kind of bird.

"A lot of people start out with kestrels," Kay said, referring to the smallest species of North American falcon. "But I'm hoping we can get a red-tail for you. A red-tail would have more game to hunt around here. Then, maybe we can work you up to something faster."

"Cool," Luther said, trying not to sound overeager.

Kay released the last pigeon and they watched Sal zoom after it. Luther's imagination zoomed right along with her, swooping into sharp turns, accelerating skyward, and plunging down in pursuit. After the last pigeon escaped Sal's talons, Kay put on the rawhide glove and called the gyr in with a loud "Hup!" She rewarded Sal with a thawed quail, but as the falcon tore apart her "prey," a fresh bank of smoke from the fires crawled across the field.

Luther took a deep breath. He thought, I wish all life was as simple as flying these birds.

Four

By the time Luther arrived home, his stepfather's black pickup and his mom's '88 white subcompact were both sitting in the drive. Even before he opened the front door, Luther could hear his mother and Vic arguing inside.

"I can't do everything," his mom was saying from the dining room as Luther entered the house. "If I'm going to work two jobs to help make ends meet, I can't shop, do the laundry, and cook every single day."

"Well, don't expect me to do it all," Luther's stepfather shouted, his face still covered with soot from a day of fighting fires. "I've been busting my butt sixteen hours a day out there, and I need you to pick up the slack."

"What slack? There hasn't been any slack in Heartwood for years. We're scraping by exactly like everyone else. At least the fires have provided some steady employment around here."

"Well, this firefighting job isn't going to last forever. Do you have to go and waste my paycheck as soon as I earn it?"

"*Waste* it!" Luther's mother exclaimed, her voice rising. "I haven't wasted a dime since we got married!"

"Did Brenda have to get the most expensive homecoming dress in Montana?" Vic asked. "And did Luther need the latest and greatest brand-name shoes? It's not like he needs them now that he's quit sports."

His parents' bickering immediately vaporized Luther's good feeling from being at Kay's. He hated it when his mom and Vic fought, and it seemed to be happening more and more often. On top of the usual money problems, the fires made everyone act like they were walking on razor wire. Luther tried to slip unnoticed past the dining room opening, but it was no go.

"Where've you been?" Vic demanded.

Luther sighed and turned toward him, a vise clenching his stomach. His stepfather stood an inch shorter than Luther and his hair showed a bit of gray, but years of handling chainsaws and tossing logs had given Vic muscles of steel. Even though Vic had never physically hit him, Luther often felt on edge around this man, especially when he was angry. Like now.

"I was working," Luther said.

"Out at that bird farm?"

"Give the boy a break," Luther's mother said, still dressed in her blue uniform from the convalescent center. "He works hard out there, and he's lucky to have a job at all in this town."

"At his age, I worked ten-hour shifts in a mill," Vic said. "*That* was work. Besides, if you add all the extra hours he spends there, he's not even making minimum wage."

"He's learning things," his mother said.

"Learning things! Like what?"

"He's learning responsibility and—"

Luther's stepfather cut her off and spoke directly to Luther. "Was it worth quitting football so you can shovel bird crap for a living? Are you just going to keep throwing away your opportunities like this?"

"Vic, *stop!*" Luther's mother yelled. She and his stepfather stood glaring at each other, jaws set.

After a pause, his mother said, "Luther, just go do your homework or something. This doesn't have anything to do with you."

Yeah, right, Luther thought as he headed to his room. He knew that all families fought sometimes, but when Vic and his mom argued like this, Luther's heart started pounding and he often broke a sweat. Brenda seemed to be able to ignore it, but it made Luther ball up his fists and want to get as far away as possible. Plenty of times he'd confided to Chet a desire to just hop a freight or hitchhike to Seattle or Minneapolis, but Chet always talked him out of it. Still, if things got much worse...

Luther sat at his desk and struggled to concentrate on his math and history assignments until his mom called him for dinner. By the time he pulled up his chair at the dining room table, his parents had called a temporary truce. His mother said grace and began passing around chicken, peas, and mashed potatoes. They ate silently for a few minutes. Finally Luther asked, "How are the fires going?"

Vic grunted and washed down a mouthful of potatoes with a swig of beer. "Looks like we're finally getting a handle on Rocky Gulch. It's going to burn a lot more trees, but the fire's 80 percent contained."

"That's great news," Luther's mom said, trying to sound cheery. Luther could tell she was forcing it. He looked at her and wished life hadn't been so rough on her. His mom and real dad had married young, right out of high school. There were a few good years, his mom told him, but Luther didn't remember them. He remembered the endless fighting, his mom having a broken nose, and, more than once, the flashing blue and red lights of the cops showing up at their old trailer.

After his mother married Vic, things had improved, at least for a while. They moved to Heartwood and bought the house. Vic was a freelance logger, cutting trees for the Apple Mountain mill, and for a while the mill had operated double-shifts, giving everyone lots of work. Soon, though, the mill started going through shutdowns. Vic picked up some work salvage logging—clearing trees that had been killed by a fire or beetles but were still usable. Overall, though, work became more and more sporadic. To make up for the lost income, his mom went back to technical school in Missoula and started working as a nurse's aid in an assisted living home. She also moonlighted providing private care to several senior citizens in town. Every year, she hoped to be able to quit, or at least cut back her hours, but work for Luther's stepfather had only grown more uncertain.

"The problem is," Vic continued, "now that we've got this fire under control, a couple of others have started up."

"Lightning?" Luther asked.

"That's what they say, but I haven't seen much lightning. I'm guessing it's job-seekers."

"Really?" Luther asked, but he knew the answer as well as anyone. Firefighting paid good money, and every year a few people were desperate enough to resort to arson to make sure they'd get a paycheck.

Vic shrugged. "In a way, I don't blame them. We wouldn't be making it right now if the Feds hadn't put me on the payroll to cut fire lines. Things are so bad around here, I bet there's not a man in town who hasn't considered using a match and can of gasoline to boost his employment prospects."

Luther stopped chewing, caught by the tone of his stepfather's voice. In Montana, arsonists were considered the lowliest of the low, but just now Vic had sounded almost, well, *sympathetic* toward them.

"But," Luther cautiously asked, "most people wouldn't ever actually start a wildfire...would they?"

Vic again shrugged. "All I know is the Forest Service is having a town meeting Thursday night to update us about the fires."

"Are you going?" Luther's mother asked him.

"Darned right I'm going. So should you. People are fed up with how this whole mess is being handled. By the way, where's Brenda?"

Oh boy, Luther thought. Here we go.

"She went to study with Samantha," his mom answered.

"That's a good one," his stepfather grumbled. "She hasn't studied since she became a cheerleader. I want that girl home for dinner from now on."

"Vic, she's eighteen. She's got a life of her own now."

"What? So we just feed and clothe her and she does what she wants?"

Luther took a last bite of chicken and stood up from the table. "Excuse me," he said, not wanting to hear his parents get into it all over again.

"Where are you going?" Vic asked.

"I've got homework."

"Go ahead, Luther," his mom said, before Vic could object.

The next morning, the smoke indeed seemed better. The morning paper reported that the Rocky Gulch blaze was finally responding to efforts to contain it. However, just like his stepfather had said, two new fires had roared through 8,000 acres in the Sapphire Range south of town and fire crews had barely touched them.

As he did every day, Luther ate his bowl of cereal for breakfast and then rode his bike to school. He ran into Chet out front. They shot the bull with a couple of other guys until the first bell and then walked to homeroom together, a class called "Current Topics." As he and Chet sat down near the back of the class, Luther noticed the new girl sitting a couple rows over to the right.

He tried to recall her name. Some boy's name, Luther

thought, like Donnie or Max. Wait. Alexandra... Alex! That's it.

Luther could only see the side of her face, but even so, he could tell he hadn't been wrong the previous day. This girl was seriously cute.

"Okay, everyone, settle down." Their teacher, Mr. Gary, stood behind his desk and opened his roll book. After a quick scan through the names, he walked around to the front of his desk and faced the students.

"As a lot of you have probably heard, tomorrow night there's going to be a town meeting right here in the high school gym. The Forest Service has called the meeting to update everyone about the fire situation and hear concerns from the community. As you can also probably guess, that's not all people are going to want to talk to the Forest Service about."

"You got that right," said Warren Juddson. "My dad's going to tear them a new—"

"Yes, as I was saying before someone interrupted me," Mr. Gary cut in, "other issues are going to be presented tomorrow night. In fact, for your homework tomorrow, I want each one of you to attend that meeting."

The class let out a chorus of groans.

"Hey, we've got a game the next night!" Warren shouted.

"Settle down," said Mr. Gary. "I'm well aware of Friday's game, but believe it or not, even you football players are here to get an education, not just play sports."

"This sucks," Warren persisted.

"You want to watch your language, Mr. Juddson?" said

Mr. Gary, his voice hardening. "You say the word, and I can drop you right out of this class. Then you can spend tomorrow and game night however you want."

"Go Mr. Gary," Luther said to himself.

"Yes *sir,*" Warren grumbled, slumping slightly.

"Good. So tomorrow night's homework is the meeting. Tonight's is to come up with at least three intelligent questions to ask at the meeting. To help you develop the questions, I thought that today in class we'd discuss the fires and why you think they're so bad this year. As you know, this is not the first time Montana's had bad fires. The 1910 blaze burned more than three million acres across the western part of the state and Idaho. In 1988, Yellowstone burned, and 1994, 1996, 2000, and 2002 were also big fire years. What's going on? Why are these fires so bad this year?"

A slender girl with straight brown hair raised her hand.

"Eliza, go ahead."

"I think the fires are happening because everything's so dry this year."

"Duh," Warren snorted. A football buddy next to him gave him a low-five.

Eliza blushed, but Mr. Gary tried to keep her talking.

"Any other reasons, Eliza?"

"I don't know," she said. "Maybe the weather patterns are changing or something."

"You mean like global warming might be giving us less rain or melting the snowpack too quickly?"

Eliza shrugged. "I heard that somewhere. Maybe. I don't know."

"Okay," said Mr. Gary, walking to the chalkboard. He wrote down "Climate Change" in big letters and then faced back toward the class.

"Mr. Juddson, you seemed to disagree with Eliza. What do you think's going on?"

Warren shrugged and stared at his hands on his desk.

"I'm sure you said something before," Mr. Gary persisted. "Why don't you share with us?"

Finally, Warren looked up. "Everyone knows why we're having these fires," he said. "It's because the Forest Service won't let us cut trees. There's too much wood out there, and now instead of us getting to use it, it's all burning up."

"So let me get this straight," Mr. Gary said. "You think the government's efforts to restrict logging on some lands have led to too much fuel in the forests and that's why we have so many fires?"

"Yeah."

Mr. Gary wrote "Forest Policies" on the board, and several kids nodded their heads. Luther wasn't surprised. He'd heard Vic complain about the very same thing. About ten years earlier, the Forest Service had declared a ban on cutting old-growth forests and a moratorium on building new logging roads throughout the West. The policies were designed to protect the country's last undamaged forest ecosystems, but they were highly unpopular in rural Montana. When the new president was elected, he decided to let each state determine how to protect its own national forest lands. Under pressure from the timber industry, most neighboring states had decided to reopen the closed

Forest Service lands to logging, but in Montana, the governor had decided to keep some protections in place. Almost everyone in Heartwood opposed the governor—especially people who came from timber industry families. Luther's stepfather was one of them.

"Anyone else have an idea about why this year's fires are so bad?" Mr. Gary asked, looking around the classroom. No one volunteered, but Mr. Gary waited. After an awkward silence, a hand went up to Luther's right. It belonged to the new girl, Alex.

Mr. Gary quickly checked his seating chart, then said, "Yes...Alexandra?"

"It's Alex," she said. Luther smiled at the correction.

"Right. Well, Alex, do you agree with Warren or Eliza?"

"I think it's the old *fire* policies that have gotten us into trouble," she said. "Not new laws to protect forests."

Mr. Gary nodded and asked, "Can you spell that out for us?"

"Well, the forests, they're used to burning every few years, and the trees are adapted to it. The fires also clean out all the underbrush, fallen limbs, and dead trees. But for the last fifty years we've been putting out every fire, so there's all this fuel built up out there. If we'd let a forest burn naturally every few years, it would be healthier and these fires wouldn't be so bad. But now there's no way we can stop them."

Luther shifted in his seat. An argument like this didn't crop up very often around Heartwood.

"Okay, Alex," Mr. Gary said as he wrote "Fire Suppression" on the board. "So you think the new forest policies are okay and the old ones got us in trouble. How did you come up with this idea?"

"I read some articles about it in a magazine," Alex answered.

"So, let's take this a bit further. These articles said that we should let the forests burn more often and that would actually make the fires less harmful?"

"Pretty much."

"But what about the huge fire of 1910 that burned three million acres?" asked Mr. Gary. "That was before fires were suppressed."

Luther thought Alex might back down, but she held her ground. "There are always going to be bad fire years," she said. "But there would be fewer of them if we burned more regularly."

Mr. Gary nodded. "Hmmm. What do the rest of you think? Does that make sense?"

"But the trees get burned up either way," another student across the room countered.

"Not necessarily," said Alex. "Ponderosa pines and larch are adapted to fire. With a regular fire, their bark gets burned, but the trees survive. The only reason they're burning and dying now is because all that extra fuel makes the fires too hot."

"That's bull!" Warren burst out.

"You want to be more specific, Warren?" Mr. Gary asked.

"Yeah, what she's saying, it's bull. Everyone knows these fires are burning because there's too many trees out there. If the government let us keep cutting the trees like we're supposed to, there wouldn't be these fires."

"So you're saying the fires are burning because of the trees?"

Luther and a few other classmates laughed. Warren gripped the edge of his desk so hard his knuckles turned white.

"What I'm saying is, they're trying to blame it on us when it's really their fault!"

Half a dozen other kids nodded and mumbled in agreement.

"Who's doing that?" asked Mr. Gary.

"The tree-huggers. The conservationalists."

Before he could think about it, Luther blurted, "It's not conservation-*al*-ists. It's conservation*ists*. And that doesn't have anything to do with what she just said."

"What do you know about it?" Warren shot back.

Luther paused. He hadn't meant to be drawn into this discussion.

"Luther?" Mr. Gary prodded.

"Well," Luther reluctantly continued, "everyone around here always blames everything on the conservationists, but we had problems here a long time before the Sierra Club showed up."

"Like what?" Mr. Gary asked.

"Well, when my stepdad started as a logger here in Heartwood, that mill ran twenty-four hours a day. Then it started shutting down a lot. That was before the Forest Service restrictions on cutting old-growth. Nobody ever seems to talk about that."

"So, why do you think the shutdowns occurred?" Mr. Gary asked.

Luther shrugged. "Everyone around here knows the reasons. The mills are more efficient than they used to be and don't need as many workers. Also, Canada's selling logs cheaper than we are. Mostly, though, we're just running out of big trees. The older mills were designed to cut large old-growth trees, and they're pretty much all gone. Instead of retooling the mills for smaller trees, it's cheaper for a lot of companies to just close up shop or scale back their operations."

"That's bull!" Warren repeated. "There's plenty of trees out there, but the government won't let us cut them."

Mr. Gary looked at Luther as if to say, "Well?"

Already, Luther regretted getting into this discussion, but he wasn't going to let Warren Juddson have the last word. "Yeah," he said, "there's a few older trees left, and we could go into every last wilderness area and untouched piece of forest and chop down every last tree we have. But then we'd still be in the exact same boat we're in now. It seems to me we should change how we do things now and still leave a few big trees for wildlife and people who want to see what an old-growth forest looks like."

After class, Luther and Chet walked down the hall toward their lockers. "Well, that was intense," Luther said, relieved that the bell had put an end to the debate.

Chet didn't say anything.

"At least it was livelier than the usual discussions," Luther added.

Chet stopped at his locker and dialed the combination. Luther saw the scowl across his friend's face. "Hey, Chet, you okay?"

His friend threw open the locker door. "Jeez, Luth, what's gotten into you?"

"Huh?" Luther asked, caught totally off guard.

Chet faced him. "You sounded like you were from the Sierra Club in there!"

"What?"

"You even made Warren Juddson look good. Just tell me it's because you were trying to impress that new girl."

"I wasn't trying to impress anyone. I said what I thought."

"That's just it, Luther. You didn't think. My dad needs that job at the mill—just like Vic needs trees to cut out there."

Luther began to recover from his shock. "I know that."

"So what? What is it?"

Luther took a breath. He lowered his voice so the girls at the next locker couldn't hear him. "Chet, come on. Do you like what's going on? People aren't working. Everyone's mad at each other. The whole state's burning up. Does that seem right?"

Chet took his math book out of his locker. "No. But we've got to stick together on this. At least I know whose side I'm on."

"So do I," Luther said defensively. "But you heard what that new girl said about how the fires should burn more often. And you can't tell me the problems at Apple

Mountain are all because of logging restrictions. Maybe we do need to make some changes around here."

"Hey, this town's already making plenty of changes, and almost all of them are hurting us." Chet picked up his backpack. "Maybe you can't wait to get out of Heartwood, but your family's still going to be here. And mine and everyone else's, too. How are they going to survive if there aren't any jobs?"

"Maybe they can start doing something else," said Luther. "Or try to get more tourists in here. Or maybe the mill can retool to cut more of the smaller trees that need to be thinned out. I don't know. But what we've been doing doesn't seem to be working anymore."

Chet stared at Luther for a full five seconds. It seemed like an hour. "Look, Luth. I tried to understand about football and wrestling and this whole bird thing. But you're wrong about this. Everyone we know is out there fighting those fires, and even if they win, there might not be any more logs for the mill. What are we going to do then?"

"I...I don't know, Chet."

"I do. We'll disappear."

Chet slammed his locker door and strode down the hall. Stunned, Luther watched him go. He knew he should go to his own locker and then to English, but he felt like he'd just been pinned by a surprise wrestling move.

Suddenly someone tapped him on the shoulder. He turned to find Alex standing next to him. "You all right?" she asked.

"I...I don't know."

"By the way, I'm Alex, but I guess you already know that. You're Luther?"

Luther stared at her and tried to shift brain gears. "Yeah, uh, Luther Wright."

Alex stuck out her hand. "Glad to meet you, Luther Wright. I just wanted to thank you for not jumping on the 'bash the conservation-al-ists' bandwagon back there."

Up close, Alex was even better looking than from a distance, but those piercing blue eyes kind of scared Luther. "I didn't do it for you," he snapped.

Alex's face stiffened and she withdrew her hand. "I know that. It's just nice to know that someone around here can carry on a conversation."

Luther felt himself rile up. "Just because we live in Heartwood, doesn't mean we're stupid."

"That's not what I meant. I meant..." Alex paused, color rising to her cheeks. "Never mind. I just wanted to thank you. For—whatever." With that, she turned and walked down the hall.

"Great job," Luther said to himself. "Zero for two."

Five

After the last bell, Luther went to the school library. He told himself he needed to work on his Current Topics assignment, but he recognized the added benefit of avoiding Chet and Alex as they left school. He still couldn't see why Chet had been so bent out of shape. Luther knew that logging issues hit close to home for almost everyone around Heartwood, but he wasn't even sure what he and Chet had been arguing about.

"And Alex," Luther said to himself. "Why'd I have to go off on her like that?"

Trying to push both incidents from his mind, Luther sat down at one of the computer terminals and began looking up websites for the Forest Service, the Montana Wilderness Alliance, the Sierra Club, and Apple Mountain Timber, the company that ran the mill and owned much of the land around Heartwood.

Each organization seemed to have a different take on the fires. The timber industry blamed the environmentalists; the environmentalists blamed the timber industry; the

Forest Service blamed fire suppression and the weather. Luther picked up his pen and began scribbling down questions. He immediately crossed out most of them because they sounded so obvious. After half an hour, he settled on three that didn't seem too lame:

1) How do wildfires affect birds of prey and other wildlife?

2) Are logged lands burning as much as lands that haven't been logged?

3) How long will it take the trees to grow back after these fires?

He slipped the questions into his notebook and headed home. After a quick stop to change his clothes and pick up Roadkill, he pedaled out to Kay's. When he arrived, he found Godzilla in the drive and Kay standing under the ponderosa pine next to the house. She was facing an easel with a large pad of drawing paper. Ten feet away Sal sat tethered on a flat perch with the hazy afternoon sun glinting off her feathers.

Luther parked his bike next to the house as Roadkill rushed over to Kay.

"Hey, Luth!" she called, lowering her drawing pen from the easel.

"Hi," he said, still knotted-up from his scrapes with Chet and Alex.

"Smoke's not as bad today, is it?"

Luther shook his head. "Sorry I'm late. Did you already feed the birds?"

"Yeah, but don't worry about it," Kay said, giving

Roadkill a head scratch. "I was just working on a sketch for my book."

Luther stepped closer to the easel and examined the drawing of Sal. Not long after they'd met, Kay had confided that she dreamed of publishing a book on American raptors, using her own drawings as illustrations. Luther knew that, after more than two years of working on the project, she'd finished the writing and most of the artwork, but he'd never actually seen her drawing a live bird.

"That's really good," he told her. Kay had packed an unbelievable amount of detail into the sketch of the gyr. After she completed the sketch, Kay would use it to do a final pen drawing. In black ink, she would not only draw the solid black lines, but would also pepper the paper with thousands of tiny dots, some placed really close together and some spread farther apart. This technique—*stippling,* she called it—gave the drawings a vivid three-dimensional look.

Kay shrugged and squinted at her work. "Thanks. It's coming out okay. After the gyrfalcon, I only have two more to do. Can you believe that? I hope someone's crazy enough to publish it."

"They will."

"We'll see. So, how was your day?"

Luther ran his fingers through his hair. "I've had better."

"You want to take Sal out and tell me about it? She's bored being a model."

"Sure," he answered, without his usual enthusiasm.

While Kay put away her easel, Luther retrieved some

strips of quail meat from the refrigerator along with a special training lure. He met Kay coming around the side of the house with Sal on her arm. He saw that she'd already attached the transmitters to Sal's jesses.

"Good. You got the lure," she said. "Sal's getting so fast, she's almost nailing those pigeons. I don't want her to start gobbling them down like doggie treats."

As they headed toward the field, Kay asked, "So Luther, what's the story?"

"About...?"

"Luther, if we're going to be friends, you can't act so dense. What's the story? From the expression on your face, it looks like a bully's just kicked sand in your face."

Luther gave a half-snort. "You should be a psychic."

As they walked out into the field, he filled Kay in on the morning's Current Topics discussion and his argument with Chet, carefully omitting his conversation with Alex after class. When he finished, Kay said, "To tell you the truth, Luther, I'm not all that surprised." She tossed Sal up in the air and the falcon sped off, doing several laps around the field before heading to her favorite perch on the dead tree snag.

"What do you mean?" Luther asked. "Why not?"

Kay began uncoiling the lure. It consisted of two dried bird wings sewn to a leather pouch. This fake "bird" was attached to a ten-foot rope and a weight so Sal couldn't fly off with the whole thing.

"Luther, don't take this the wrong way," Kay said, "but you're different from most people around here. Sure, you come from the same background as everyone else, but you see things that other people don't." She began swinging the lure in big circles around her head. "Hup! Hup! Hup!" she called.

Sal hunched on her perch and watched.

"Come on, baby," Kay said in a low voice. She swung the lure through two more rotations, calling "Hup!" each time, and suddenly Sal dove off the perch. The bird darted straight for the lure, coming within inches before Kay whisked it away, shouting "Ho!"

When Luther first started working with Kay, she explained that the "Hup!" got Sal's attention while the "Ho!" signaled that prey was still available—useful signals when they finally got to take Sal out for a real hunt.

As Kay continued to swing the lure, Sal banked right, did a full loop, and then dove, or *stooped,* down on it again. Once more, the falcon came within inches before Kay jerked the lure away with another "Ho!"

Kay repeated the maneuver about twenty times. When she sensed Sal getting tired, Kay let the falcon connect with the lure and take it to the ground.

"Good girl," Kay said, slowly approaching the falcon. She sat on the ground next to Sal and fed her a small piece of quail as a reward.

"I never get tired of watching her fly," Luther said, squatting down beside Kay. She passed him a piece of quail to give to Roadkill, who crouched a few feet away, wagging his tail.

"Yeah," Kay crooned to the bird. "You did real good, didn't you, girl?" She fed Sal another strip of meat. "Anyway, what I was saying, Luther, is that you're a step ahead of a lot of people. When I first showed you the birds, you asked all kinds of questions about them. Good questions."

"Doesn't everyone?"

"Some do," Kay said. "But you'd be surprised how many people just aren't that interested."

"How could they not be?"

"A lot of people are too tired to think about things outside themselves, I guess. Or maybe some people are just born curious and some aren't. Anyway, it doesn't surprise me that you're going to butt heads with a few people around Heartwood—especially if you start challenging the status quo."

"I'm not trying to be different," he told Kay, anxiety needling his brain.

"I know. But we all are who we are. Do you think I fit the mold back in Louisiana?"

Luther had never thought about it. "I don't know."

"Well, I didn't," Kay said. "I was the Class A, Number One Freakazoid where I grew up. I took a lot of crap, but I wouldn't change a thing, because look at this." Kay motioned her hand at the landscape around her. "Who could ask for a better life than working with wild animals in the greatest place on earth?"

Luther digested Kay's words and the knots in his stomach loosened.

After a few moments, he asked, "Kay? Do you know the new Fish and Wildlife guy? I think his last name is Matthews or something."

"Trent? Sure, I know Trent." Kay stood up with Sal on her hand. "He's a good man. He's going to be at the Forest Service meeting tomorrow night. You going?"

"Yeah," said Luther, straightening up. "It's a class assignment."

Kay laughed and brushed a strand of hair from her face. "Well, assigned or not, it ought to be good entertainment. That's one of the things I worked on earlier today. Trent and the Forest Service guys asked me to put together some information in case anyone asks about how the fires affect raptors and farm animals."

"That's weird. We had to make up some questions for the meeting and that's the first one I wrote down."

As they approached the falcon house, Kay turned to Luther. "So why'd you ask about Trent Matthews?"

"I don't know. His daughter's in my Current Topics class. She's the one who got everyone fired up in class today."

"Ah," Kay said, raising her eyebrows. "And she's pretty good-looking, too, isn't she?"

Luther looked away. "No...I mean...she's okay."

"Have it your way, Luth," Kay said with a laugh. "I gotta tell you, though, I'm impressed. You've got much better taste in women than I gave you credit for."

The next day, Luther avoided people as much as possible. He said hi to Chet, but his friend turned away and started talking to some other football guys. During lunch and after school, Luther laid low in the library and then rode his bike straight home. Kay had given him the afternoon off, so instead of riding out to feed the birds, he threw sticks for Roadkill and tackled his homework before heading to the Forest Service meeting.

When Luther walked into the gym, it was already more than half full. It seemed like the entire town of Heartwood, not to mention most of the high school students and staff, had turned out for the big showdown. Searching the crowd, he saw Alex sitting off by herself. Then, at the far end of the bleachers, he spotted Chet and many of his former football and wrestling teammates. Right in the middle of the group sat the hulking form of Warren Juddson.

Seeing Warren and his teammates together made Luther replay the events of the last season—especially what had happened after the final game. *If I'd made a different decision then, I might be sitting with everyone else now.*

But he'd never get that moment to do over again. And for the hundredth time since that night, the sour tastes of guilt and regret filled his mouth.

He turned his eyes away from his ex-teammates and chose an empty seat in one of the higher bleachers off to the side, where he could watch without being noticed. People continued to stream into the gym. Among them were Kay and, a few minutes later, his stepfather, still dressed in his firefighting clothes. Luther also recognized the CEO of Apple Mountain Timber, along with three or four of the company's other executives. A din of lively chatter echoed off the gymnasium walls.

At ten past seven, Heartwood's mayor, the Honorable Marty Williams, stepped up to the mike on the gym floor and cleared his throat. "If we can get started…"

The large room began to quiet as people shifted their attention to the mayor. A dozen or so people sat in folding chairs on either side of him. Luther identified Forest Service uniforms on some of them. Others dressed casually in jeans and work shirts.

"Thank you," said the mayor, holding up his hands to further quiet the crowd. "Thank you. We'd like to get started. As you all know, we called this meeting to update you on current fire conditions, the fire outlook for the next several weeks, and preparations that have been made in case a fire threatens Heartwood directly. Here to speak with us is Chip Powers, the director of the U.S. Forest Service's Northern Region. Please welcome him."

A smattering of applause greeted the director as he approached the mike. This will be interesting, Luther thought.

"Thank you," Mr. Powers said. "And thank you all for coming out tonight. These have been difficult weeks for everyone, I know, but I appreciate the spirit of cooperation everyone in Heartwood has shown in getting this situation under control."

Luther heard a few grumbles from the crowd.

"What I'd like to do first is give you an update on the fire situation in western Montana," Mr. Powers began, referring to some papers in his hands. "Currently, sixteen wildfires are burning, ranging in size from just over three acres to more than 130,000 acres. As most of you know, local, state, federal, and private agencies are cooperating to contain the most dangerous of these blazes. More than 12,000 firefighters are working around the clock in Montana alone. Unfortunately, extremely hot, dry conditions continue to dominate our region. In the absence of rain or cooler weather, we don't foresee the situation improving for at least two to three weeks."

As Luther listened, he noticed a group of four men enter the gym. They all wore plaid jackets or beige Carhartts, but one of them stood out. Everyone in Heartwood recognized the red hair and bullying swagger of Warren's father, Knot Juddson. With Knot walked Warren's brother Raymond.

Luther smelled trouble.

"Now, since we are obviously overwhelmed by the magnitude of these blazes," the Forest Service director continued, "we've placed our first priority on saving people's lives, both the firefighters' and the general public's. Next priority is given to protecting houses, businesses, and finally, timberlands."

"How about protecting our jobs?" someone suddenly shouted.

The mayor stepped in. "If we can save questions and comments until the end—"

"No, it's okay," said Mr. Powers. "I know that many of you are very concerned by the loss of timber in the forests, and I'd like to address that now."

"It's about time," someone muttered loudly.

"As you all know, fire is part of the natural cycle of forests all over the West. Many of the forests need fire to survive and—"

Knot Juddson suddenly leaped to his feet and shouted, "Then why are the trees burning down to the ground? You call that surviving?"

"And what about our homes?" someone else added. "Are you going to let them burn too?"

People grumbled in agreement.

They aren't even listening, Luther thought.

"While you talk your eco-politics," Knot stormed on, "our futures are burning up out there!"

Mr. Powers stayed calm. "I appreciate your concern—"

"I don't think you do!" Knot shouted. "First, you went and closed down the forests—*our* forests—and now you're letting them burn right before our eyes."

"That's right!" someone yelled, and half the people in the audience shouted their agreement. Luther wondered if his stepfather's voice was among them.

"If you'd give me a chance to speak, I'd like to take these issues one at a time," said Mr. Powers. The protests quieted to a low murmur. "First of all, about half of the acreage affected by the fires is on private lands, not public forests. Much of the land burning around Heartwood belongs to Apple Mountain Timber Company, and we're working closely with them to contain the blazes. Second, as I hope most of you know, only a small percentage of Montana's national forests have been closed to logging. Of those closed areas, very few are burning. Even though a disproportionate number of the newer fires seem to have erupted in roadless areas, fires still have affected only about 3 percent of the logging closure areas on national forest lands—"

"That's a load of crap!" Knot Juddson yelled. "You're just saying this to protect your asses. Everyone in this room knows that without those extra trees out there—trees that should have been logged—these fires would be out already!"

The crowd erupted into applause that continued for almost a minute.

"Please!" the mayor shouted. "Let's try to keep this discussion orderly."

When the noise began to die down, Mr. Powers continued. "I understand how you feel, but what you say is just not borne out by the facts. This year, the number of trees on the land seems to bear almost no relation to—"

"This is bullcrap!" Knot interrupted, angrily stabbing his finger in the direction of the Forest Service director. "The government is stealing our livelihoods and then telling us they have nothing to do with it. While they caved in to the tree-hugging, left-wing environmentalists, we could have been out there cutting trees, saving our jobs, and saving our town!"

Knot turned to face the crowd. "Do we have to listen to these lies?"

"NO!" the crowd shouted back.

"Well then, let's show them where they can shove their logging restrictions and forest closures!" To a chorus of cheers, Knot stormed out of the building. Raymond,

Warren, and about fifty more people—almost all of them mill workers, loggers, and their families—stood and followed. Luther closely watched his stepfather. Though Vic had clapped at what Knot said, he stopped short of following him out of the building.

Stunned, the Forest Service director and the mayor looked at each other blankly, unsure what to do next. Luther glanced over at the Apple Mountain officers. They were smiling and whispering to one another. They stood and joined Knot and the other walkouts.

Mayor Williams and Mr. Powers quickly conferred, and then the mayor stepped to the mike. "Given the circumstances, we're going to call this meeting short. If anyone would like to ask questions one-on-one with Mr. Powers or any of the other people who volunteered their time tonight, they have agreed to stay behind for a few minutes. Otherwise, we will post information in the *Heartwood Reporter* as events develop. Thank you."

Those who remained burst into loud talking and rose to leave the building. As they filed out, Luther looked to the front of the gym and saw that only three or four people had approached the Forest Service reps with questions.

What the heck, Luther thought. He stood and made his way to where the mayor and Forest Service director stood.

The mayor noticed Luther and stuck out his hand. "You're Vic's son, aren't you?"

"Yes, sir. My name's Luther."

"Glad you could make it," said the mayor. Then he paused and chuckled. "Though I'm not sure you witnessed the best example of democracy in action."

"Oh, I don't know," the Forest Service director wryly commented. "It was a perfect example of hijacking one meeting to push another agenda."

Luther pulled his list from his pocket.

"Do you have a question?" the mayor asked him.

"Yeah, uh, for Mr. Powers."

The Forest Service director looked surprised. "Oh, sure. Fire away—I mean, go ahead."

"I was just wondering about something you said."

"Okay."

"You, uh, mentioned that there are only a few fires burning in the closure areas—the places where logging is restricted to protect old-growth forests. Is that right?"

"That's correct."

"Well, does that mean that most of the fires are burning in places that have already been logged?"

Mr. Powers looked at the mayor. "That's the kind of question I hoped for earlier." Turning back to Luther, he answered, "Yes, that's right. The fires are burning *everywhere*. It doesn't seem to matter whether an area's been clear-cut, selectively logged, or kept from being logged altogether. Conditions are so dry this year that everything's burning. But as I mentioned, there seem to be more of the newer fires on the protected lands. We suspect most of them are set by arsonists, but we're not sure just yet."

"But overall," Luther pressed, "restrictions on cutting the older, bigger trees don't have anything to do with the forest fires?"

"We won't know for sure until the season's all over, but

yes, I'd say that's true. This year it's all burning, but I'll tell you one more thing. Some of the hottest blazes have actually been in areas that were logged recently."

That surprised Luther. "Why?"

"Well, logging generates a lot of slash—you know what that is?"

Luther nodded. "The branches and bark and stuff that's left behind from logging."

"Right. That slash just turns into a tinderbox. We had one case where flames shot more than 200 feet into the air—from a plot that had been completely cleared of trees! The sparks from the blaze flew over into a neighboring plot of forested land and before we knew it, that blew up, too."

Mayor Williams picked up his coat from the back of his chair. "Did you have any other questions?" he asked.

Luther glanced around and noticed that the gym had almost emptied. "Yeah, I did," he said. "I wondered how the fires are affecting wildlife."

"Hmm. That's a tough one," said the Forest Service director. "But it appears that most wildlife can handle the fires pretty well. Deer, elk, and other big animals simply get out of the way. Some smaller animals are killed, and some habitats destroyed. But in the long run the fires are good for wildlife."

"You mean because they leave dead snags for the birds to nest in?" Luther asked.

Mr. Powers seemed impressed. "Yes. That's right. Black-backed woodpeckers, for instance, live almost exclusively in freshly burned areas. Also, the plant diversity is often much higher after a fire and that feeds a greater variety of insects, birds, and other animals. So while in the short run, the fires may impact a lot of species, in the long run, the fires actually help most kinds of wildlife.

"And," the director added with a smile, "no one is happier about fires than mushroom pickers. Mushrooms go crazy after a burn. There's going to be bumper crops of morels the next few years."

"Thank you," said Luther, shaking hands with both Mr. Powers and the mayor.

Luther glanced around for Kay so he could say hello, but she'd apparently left already, so he headed through the bleachers to the exit. When he stepped outside, the sun sat low and blazing orange on the horizon. Long purple smoke clouds stretched to the west, and Luther's nose filled with the smell of ash. The last cars, packed with people from the meeting, were just leaving the school parking lot when Luther spotted a familiar figure sitting on the low wall in front of the school.

uther briefly considered walking past Alex without saying anything, but then told himself, "That's stupid. Just suck it up."

She appeared to be watching the sunset, but turned her head as Luther approached. He noticed that her hair no longer hung in a ponytail but flowed over her shoulders like gleaming copper.

"Hi," said Luther.

"Hi."

"So you…uh…came to the meeting?"

Alex nodded.

Luther stood a moment, hands in his pockets. "So, what are you doing?"

Alex sat stiffly. "Just waiting for my dad. He's inside, talking with the Forest Service guys."

"Oh yeah. I heard he came to answer questions." Luther shifted his weight from his left to his right foot, fighting the urge to flee. "Look, I'm…uh…really sorry for yesterday."

Alex flipped her hair to one side. "It's no big deal."

"What I mean is, it didn't have anything to do with you. It was something else."

"You don't have to explain."

"I know. It's this whole fire thing. I guess I'm not..." Luther fumbled, searching for the words he wanted. "Anyway, what I meant was—"

"You're not fitting in anymore?" Alex asked, staring straight at him.

Surprised, Luther looked into her intense blue eyes. That wasn't what he was going to say, but it hit home. "Yeah," he said.

Alex stood up. "You'll get used to it. Anyway, there's my dad. See you tomorrow."

"Yeah, see you."

When Luther got up the next morning, his mom and Vic had already left for work. Brenda had spent the night at Sam's, so Luther sat alone at the kitchen table, eating his usual bowl of cereal and reading the *Heartwood Reporter*. The local newspaper usually came out only three days a week. During the fires, though, they'd been publishing extra issues, and no surprise, this edition focused on last night's Forest Service meeting. "Public Fed Up!" the headline read. The article gave a blow-by-blow account of people's objections to the Forest Service logging policies with a heavy focus on the idea that the government was responsible for the fires. To the right of the text, a photo of an angry Knot Juddson burst from the page.

"Idiot," Luther muttered to himself. Scanning the rest of the paper, he could find nothing on the Forest Service's descriptions of which lands were burning, how the clear-cuts had contributed to the fire danger, and the long-term benefits of the fires. In a way, that didn't surprise him. Though Apple Mountain Timber didn't technically own the *Reporter,* Luther knew as well as anyone that the paper served as a mouthpiece for the company. The newspaper wouldn't dare publish a story Apple Mountain might find objectionable. What Luther didn't understand was why accurate stories about the fires would be objectionable to Apple Mountain. Wouldn't a complete understanding of why the fires were happening benefit the company as much as anyone else? Why was everyone just focusing on the road closures and logging restrictions instead of trying to get a handle on the big picture?

Luther didn't have time to ponder these questions. Five minutes before the first bell, he swallowed his last mouthful of cereal, picked up his backpack, and raced to school. Still breathing hard, he parked his bike and walked to Current Topics. Alex gave him a brief smile as he made his way to his desk and he nodded back. As he had the day before, Chet turned away and began talking with some of the other players about tonight's football game. A moment later, Warren Juddson strutted into class, several other football players in tow.

"My dad kicked their asses last night," Warren Juddson boasted to his audience. "He put 'em right in their places and told 'em where they could shove their policies. Those damned eco-freaks didn't have a chance."

As Warren talked, his gaze shifted directly toward Alex and then at Luther. Some kids laughed and gave Warren high fives as he made his way to his desk.

After Mr. Gary took roll, he asked the class about the previous night's meeting. Unlike the previous day, the students needed no prompting. Several of them leaped in, bashing the Forest Service in general and environmentalists in particular. One girl mentioned that the Forest Service had hardly been given a chance to speak, but Warren and his supporters quickly drowned her out. Luther kept his mouth shut—and noticed Alex did, too. The more Luther listened, though, the more he felt like people were off on the wrong track. They're not really looking at what's going on, he thought. They're just looking for someone to blame.

When the bell rang for the next class, Luther hurried to his locker to get his math book. When he turned around, he saw Alex walking toward him.

"Hey," he said.

"Hi."

Luther noticed that she'd tied her hair in a ponytail again and wondered why she did that. He liked it down a lot better, like she'd worn it the night before.

"How are you?" he asked.

"I'm okay," she answered. "You were quiet in there."

Luther shrugged. "Didn't really have anything to say."

"I doubt *that*."

Luther smiled. "You weren't exactly chattering away yourself."

"No."

They stood for a moment, reading the floor tiles and glancing down the hall. "What class you got now?" Luther finally asked.

"Spanish. You?"

"Math. Advanced algebra."

"You're not one of those nerdy math types are you?"

"You mean like a nerdy Spanish type?"

Alex suppressed a smile. "Touché."

"Well, I'd better get going," Luther said, closing his locker door.

"Do you like horses?"

He stopped and turned back toward her. "What do you mean? To eat?"

Alex laughed out loud, and Luther noticed that her left cheek dimpled.

"No," she said, "to *ride*."

Luther could count on one hand the number of times he'd ridden a horse, but he said, "Yeah, they're okay."

"Well, I know you're probably going to the pep rally and the game, but I...I was wondering if you felt like riding this afternoon."

"Where are we going to get the horses?"

The warning bell for the next period blasted.

"Oops. We're going to be late," Alex said.

Luther shrugged. "I don't care." It was a lie, but how often did he get to talk to someone as good-looking as Alex?

"Me neither," Alex said. "Anyway, I've got two horses."

"You have *two?*"

"Well, one's my dad's. I'll ride his and you can ride mine. She's easier."

Luther didn't know whether or not to take that as an insult. "That sounds okay."

"Well, uh..." Suddenly Alex looked nervous. "But you're probably going to the game."

Luther took a deep breath. "No. I was going to, but I don't think I'm exactly welcome there anymore."

Alex's head cocked slightly to the side. "No? Why not?"

Luther fingered the lock on his closed locker. "It's complicated." After a pause, he continued. "Anyway, I'm busy for about an hour after school. Will that be too late? For riding, I mean?"

"No, I have to go out and get the horses groomed and saddled anyway."

Luther raised his eyebrows. "You do that by yourself?"

By now the halls had emptied and Alex's laugh echoed off the locker-lined walls. "Sure," she answered. "I know how to brush my own teeth and dress myself, too."

"Very funny," Luther said, but he appreciated the quick-witted reply.

Alex asked, "You know where the Heartwood Stables are?"

"Out on the old highway?"

"That's the place. Why don't you meet me there when you're finished working?"

Luther nodded. "Sounds good. See you then."

"See you."

☙

After school, Luther rushed home, changed into his work clothes, and then remounted his ten-speed. "Roadkill, stay!" he shouted. The Border collie's ears fell in disappointment, and Luther's chest twanged with guilt. "We'll go tomorrow for sure," he told the dog.

He left his house in high gear and pedaled hard for Kay's. Fresh smoke from the Sapphire blazes made him cough as he rode, but he reached the farm in record time. Thankfully, Godzilla was missing from the drive. Luther liked talking to Kay and knew she'd have a lot to say about last night's meeting, but today he wanted to finish his chores and get out of there. He quickly fed the birds and had just hopped onto his bike again when Kay's green International rumbled down the drive.

"Hey, where are you off to?" Kay shouted through the driver's side window. "You decide to go to the game tonight?"

Luther wheeled over to her. "No. Something else came up," he said, avoiding her eyes.

"Everything all right?"

"Yeah. I mean, sure. No problem."

"Where's Roadkill?"

"I left him at home. I've got to go somewhere else. Anyway, the birds are all fed. I'll see you in the morning."

"Okay. Sure," Kay said, suppressing a grin. "Thanks."

"No problem!" Luther yelled as he pedaled away.

After recrossing the rail-car bridge under the cottonwoods, Luther turned right, off onto a dusty path that was a shortcut to the old highway. His bike rattled and clanked as he dodged potholes and swerved around clumps of sage and knapweed. He crossed the Montana Rail Link tracks and then paralleled a small creek that flowed into the Clark Fork River. As the path approached a rutted dirt road that led down to the creek, Luther suddenly braked and stopped. Up ahead, through a tangle of cottonwoods and willows, he saw what looked like his stepfather's black pickup truck. A few yards in front of the truck, Vic was talking to another man Luther only vaguely recognized.

He wasn't sure why, but something didn't feel right about seeing them there. Vic was supposed to be off fighting fires, but it was more than that. Instinctively, Luther laid down his bicycle and quietly crept forward, careful to stay hidden by trees. At first, the roar of the creek drowned the men's conversation, but as Luther moved closer, he began catching words and scraps of sentences.

"…easy…thing to do…," the other man said. Up close, Luther recognized him as one of the independent loggers Vic used to work with. His name was Henry or Hank or something.

Then, his stepfather spoke. "…worth the risk…prefer kerosene…"

Luther's heart started hammering. *Did Vic just say kerosene?*

He strained to hear more, but the blasts from a passing freight train obliterated their voices. By the time the train had rumbled past, his stepfather and Hank—or whoever—had climbed back into the pickup. Vic started it up, turned it around, and headed out to the road.

Luther hands were shaking as he picked up his bike. In his head, he repeated the words he had overheard. What do they mean? he wondered. Is it possible Vic is somehow involved with these fires?

Suddenly Luther recalled their conversation around the dinner table a couple of nights earlier. *Vic said he could understand why someone would start a fire. He almost sounded like he'd do it himself under the right conditions.*

But then, Luther shook his head. "Forget it," he muttered. "Vic is a logger. He'd never intentionally destroy a forest."

Still, a nagging feeling clung to him as he climbed back onto his bike and pedaled the last few hundred yards to the old highway.

Luther had never actually been to Heartwood Stables, but he'd passed them dozens, if not hundreds, of times. They sat on ten acres nestled up to the base of the mountains, about three miles east of town. As he turned into the drive, Luther asked himself if he really wanted to be doing this. After all, he didn't know Alex very well and her intense blue eyes still made him nervous. It was too late to back out now, though. He'd feel like an idiot if she saw him pedaling away again, so he parked his bike next to an enormous barn with a metal roof and looked around.

A line of ponderosa pines grew behind the barn and along the edge of the parking area. On the other side of the parking area, a dozen or so horses searched for dry grass in several large, open pens. In one of them, a woman jumped a gray spotted horse over barrels and fences. Luther didn't see Alex anywhere, so he entered the barn. To his left, fluorescent lights glared over a large, indoor riding arena. To the right, a long row of stalls lined the wall. Outside one of these, Luther saw a brown mare with white feet, saddled and tethered to a rail. Luther walked toward it and, hearing a voice, peered into the adjacent stable.

"Come on," Alex pleaded with a tall black gelding. She was bent over, facing away from Luther, trying to clean the dirt from one of the horse's front hooves. The horse wasn't cooperating and kept pulling his foot away. Luther took the opportunity to admire the fit of Alex's jeans. Nice view, he thought.

"Stop it, darn you!" Alex said, exasperated. Finally, the horse obeyed.

"Are horses always this much fun?" Luther asked.

Alex dropped the hoof and bolted straight up, whacking her head against the horse's rib cage. Luther noticed her freckled face darken to pink.

"Oh, I didn't expect you for a while," Alex said. "I'm not quite done getting Diamond here ready."

"I got through my chores faster than I expected," Luther explained, trying to slow his breathing from the bike ride and tame the jitters in his stomach. "Need any help?"

The gelding picked up its hooves and shuffled to one side.

"I got it, but you seem to be making Diamond nervous. Maybe you could wait out there with Sugar until I'm finished with this?"

"Sure," said Luther, backing up.

He walked over to the brown mare, but unlike the gelding, the smaller horse ignored him. Luther had never spent much time around horses and he wasn't sure how to act.

"How're you doing?" he asked the mare.

Sugar didn't move and Luther stepped closer.

"You're a pretty horse, aren't you?"

Again, the mare didn't respond, so Luther stepped right up next to the horse's head. He reached out slowly and stroked the horse's long forehead between her eyes.

"That's a good horse," he said. "Are we going to be friends?"

Suddenly, Sugar shook her head and made a loud flapping sound with her lips. Luther leaped back, tripped over a hay bale, and landed flat on his butt.

"Quite...a way you have with animals," Alex said from behind him. He looked over his shoulder to see her laughing so hard she could barely talk.

This time it was Luther's face that flushed crimson. "Your horse attacked me!"

"She...she wasn't attacking you!" Alex laughed, still struggling for breath.

Luther got up and brushed straw from his backside. "She was going to. Didn't you hear her growl at me?"

Composing herself at last, Alex walked over to the mare and stroked her under the neck. "Horses don't growl. She just breathed out to relax. I think she likes you."

Luther wasn't so sure, but he stepped closer and put his hand lightly on the horse's neck.

"See?" Alex said. "She's a pushover."

"I'm not riding *her,* am I?" Luther asked, his voice cracking.

"Believe me," Alex said, sweeping her hair over her shoulder, "this is the horse you want to ride. Diamond can be a handful, even for me."

"Well..."

"Come on. You'll see."

Alex went back to the stall and led Diamond out, his black coat gleaming under the fluorescent lights. Luther noticed that the gelding stood noticeably taller than Sugar.

"Untie Sugar and take hold of her lead," Alex instructed.

Still cautious, Luther untied the mare. He took a step and gently pulled on the leather straps. Sugar followed obligingly.

"This way," Alex motioned, leading Diamond toward the barn door. As she walked, she explained, "Diamond's a thoroughbred and a bit high-strung. Sugar's a quarter horse. They tend to be a lot mellower, even though she's a mare."

"What do you mean?"

"Well, in general geldings are easier to handle than mares, but it's not a hard-and-fast rule. Sugar's a great horse for a beginning rider."

They walked out into the hazy sunshine. "Hey, why aren't there more people around?" Luther asked. "It looks like there are plenty of horses."

Alex stopped and stroked Diamond's cheek. "Most people come to ride later, after they get off work. The owner lives farther out of town, east of here. She's usually here in the mornings and goes home when I get here."

"So you're here alone in the afternoons?"

"A night manager comes in from six until closing, but yeah. I guess I'm the afternoon shift. You need a leg up?"

Luther studied the stirrups and saddle. "I think I remember how to do this."

"Take the reins in your left hand and grab the saddle horn with the same hand. Stick your left foot in the left stirrup and throw your right leg over."

"Will it scare her? I think someone held the last horse I got on."

"No. She'll be fine."

Luther followed Alex's instructions and tried to swing his leg over the mare's back, but the horse stood taller than he had estimated and he stepped back onto the ground. He tried again, pushing off with more force, and suddenly found himself in the saddle.

"Good job," Alex said. In a single fluid movement, she hoisted herself into Diamond's saddle. Watching her move, Luther felt a light tingling in his chest.

"Where are we going?" he asked, trying to sound casual.

"They've closed all the forest trails because of the fires, so we'll have to go along the river." Alex made a couple of clicking sounds with her tongue, and Diamond walked toward the highway. Luther gave a little kick with his heels and Sugar followed.

Seven

Luther and Alex crossed the highway onto a trail that led through cottonwoods and willows. Both horses seemed to know where to go, and Luther hardly touched the reins.

"Have you been down here before?" Alex asked, turning partway around.

Luther liked how she looked, sitting straight and confident in the saddle. "We used to ride our bikes here before they closed it to everything except horses and people," he said.

"Did that make you mad?"

Luther laughed. "Yeah. We didn't think the place ought to be just for horse-riders and bird-watchers."

"Oh, I *see*."

"On the other hand, the animals are probably a lot happier that we're gone. We made a lot of noise and were always flushing deer and scaring birds." Luther ducked under a low cottonwood branch. "So you brought these horses over from Billings?"

"Both of them. How'd you know I came from Billings?"

Luther smiled. "Heartwood's a pretty small place."

"So I'm learning," Alex said. "In Billings, we kept them on our own property north of town. We had about five acres, so that made it real easy."

"Why don't you get a place here?"

"My dad wants to see how we like it first. He's heard this can be a tough place for a Fish and Wildlife officer."

"Why's that?" Luther asked, already guessing the answer.

"Well, there's a lot of poaching around here, and people aren't too fond of government people sticking their noses in."

"Some people hunt out of season. But I think most people in Heartwood want to do the right thing. My stepdad hates poachers."

Alex looked at him over her shoulder. "Would he turn one in if he knew the guy?"

Her question made him think about the meeting he'd witnessed a half-hour earlier with Vic and that other man. He debated mentioning it to Alex, but decided it was probably nothing anyway. "I don't know."

"Well, that's the problem," Alex said, her voice rising. "It's almost impossible to catch someone around here because everyone else covers for them."

Luther didn't want to believe that was true, but he thought about the dead raptors that had been brought to Kay's lately. *Surely somebody knows who's shooting them.*

"Is it expensive to board horses here?" Luther asked, changing subjects.

Alex pushed an overhanging branch to the side. "Look out for this."

Luther leaned to the left. "Got it."

"It's expensive, but I work at the stables about fifteen hours a week in exchange for Sugar's board."

"You have time to do that with school?"

"Do you? I hear you work after school, too."

"Who told you that?"

Alex smiled back at him, her dimple again showing. "Heartwood's a pretty small place."

Luther laughed. "Touché, as you'd say."

"You work with Dr. Benaton?"

Luther was so used to calling Kay by her first name that her doctor name caught him by surprise. "Yeah, at Kay's place."

"What do you do there?"

They reached a wide stretch on the trail where the river rushed below them. Sugar sidled up next to Diamond.

"Anything she wants me to. Clean out cages, feed the birds. Sometimes I fix things."

"Like what?"

Luther swatted at a horsefly. "Little stuff. If a door comes off its hinges or something, I put it back on. Sometimes I build cages."

"How'd you learn to do that?"

Luther liked how impressed Alex sounded. "Vic—my stepfather—taught me mostly. He built most of our house and used to have me help him a lot. It's pretty easy."

"It doesn't sound easy."

They stopped talking as the horses climbed a small knoll that overlooked the river and gave them a view of the mountains beyond. A large black and white bird approached less than fifty feet above their heads. It seemed to be checking out the two horses before it resumed looking for fish.

Luther pointed. "Osprey."

"Wow, look at him," Alex said. "I love this spot. Even on a hazy day like this, you always see something interesting."

Luther and Alex let the horses browse as they gazed out over the river. The sun burned orange through the smoky sky and seemed to set the river on fire where it curved south. From this high point, Luther could see some of the cottonwoods growing near Kay's place, a mile or so downstream. He took a deep breath and suddenly felt the same way here that he felt working with the birds. Light. Free, somehow.

"Are you sorry you're not going to the game tonight?" Alex asked, turning to him.

Luther kept his eyes on the horizon. "Yeah. A little."

"Tell me if this is none of my business, but someone told me you played last year and were really good. Why'd you quit?"

"Everyone asks me that."

"Sorry to be predictable."

Luther gave a small wave of his hand and bent over to stroke the side of Sugar's neck. The muscles in her neck felt like cords of iron or steel, and he liked the dusty smell of horse that reached his nostrils. "I tell most people it's because I got a job."

"It's not?"

Luther's mind veered back to the freshmen team's final game ten months before—and what had happened afterward. *How could I explain it to her?*

"You okay?"

Luther's eyes snapped to Alex. "Um, yeah, sorry."

"You don't have to talk about it if you don't want to."

He met her steady gaze. Part of him did want to talk to someone, but he wondered if she would understand. No one else in Heartwood seemed to get what his problem was, but Alex just might.

"Something happened last year," he said, "after our last game of the season."

"Oh?"

Luther hesitated and said, "Um, yeah. Sort of. It wasn't only that...thing. What happened just made me see stuff I hadn't seen before."

Alex leaned forward in her saddle. "Did you lose the game or something? Were you disappointed?"

Luther nodded. "Yeah, we lost. Afterward, there was this big party that got out of hand."

"Were a lot of people drinking? Having wild sex?"

"Yeah," Luther said, distracted. "I mean about the drinking part."

"And?"

Luther again paused and finally said, "It's hard to explain."

"Oh." Alex waited for him to go on. When he didn't, she asked, "Do you miss playing football?"

Luther shrugged. "A lot of it," he said, taking a deep breath. "I miss the guys, mostly. Being part of something. I mean, I used to be just like Chet and everyone else— even Warren."

"Oh come on!" Alex said. "Warren Juddson?"

Luther smiled. "Well, maybe not exactly like him. But we all used to do the same stuff—just messing around, going out to shoot squirrels, that sort of thing. I even hung out with Warren the first year or two I lived in Heartwood. And the thing is, I had a lot of fun. But after that last game, I just started thinking it was stupid to spend all my time partying and goofing around. You know what I mean?"

Alex picked a burr from Diamond's mane. "I think so."

Luther knew he wasn't telling Alex the whole story. He figured she knew it, too, but he appreciated that she wasn't pressing him more. Instead, she asked, "And you were good at it? Football, I mean?"

"Well, yeah. I was pretty good. And I liked it, too. At least I liked the attention. But the thing is, once I started working at Kay's, I realized that I liked *that* even more than sports. Everyone else said I should stick with football, but after a couple of weeks working with the birds, I realized that that was more...who I really was."

"What does your family think?"

He looked at her. "You sure ask a lot of questions."

Alex laughed, the dimple again denting her cheek. "I know. My dad's always complaining how nosy I am. Just tell me to shut up and I will."

"No, it's okay. My stepfather thinks I'm crazy for quitting the team. He used to say football and wrestling would be my ticket out of Heartwood, that maybe I could even get a scholarship to play at U of M or Montana Western. But since I dropped out, I feel like he doesn't even want me around anymore. My mom doesn't mind so much, but my stepsister pretty much thinks the same way Vic does."

"Your friends?"

Luther sighed. The heaviness he'd almost forgotten for the last few hours settled back into his chest. "I don't think most of them get it. It's not like they hate me or anything, but I know some of the guys think I betrayed the team. And even if I still wanted to hang out with them, without football we don't have much in common. I mean, they're at practice or games all the time, and I work out at Kay's, so our paths don't really cross that much outside of school.

"Chet and I were getting along okay," Luther went on, "before this whole forest fire stuff came up. Now even he seems to be avoiding me."

"You haven't done anything wrong," said Alex. "With the forest stuff, I mean."

Luther shifted in his saddle. "Sometimes I'm not so sure. It's just that I don't get what's happening. Anyone can see that logging is on its way out around here — at least the way it used to be. All the best timber's been cut, and with the new milling machines, they don't need as many workers anyway. Apple Mountain should've seen this coming twenty years ago and slowed things down so there'd be steadier work now. Instead, they just blame the government for trying to protect what's left."

The osprey returned, flying past them in the opposite direction, a fourteen-inch trout clutched in its talons.

Luther watched until the bird flew beyond a line of trees. "But if someone opens his mouth to talk about it," he continued, "everyone else calls him a traitor and tells him he's on the wrong side. You know? I mean, like at that meeting last night. The Forest Service had a lot of good things to say—things everyone in Heartwood should be thinking about. But the Forest Service guys didn't even get a chance to talk."

"Well," Alex said, fingering a leather necklace she wore around her neck, "if it makes you feel any better, Billings was the same way sometimes. There, the debate wasn't about timber. It was about coal and gas exploration, and pollution from oil refineries."

"Really?"

"Yeah. Seems like when people's jobs are at stake, they stop thinking clearly—even if a change would help them later on."

"But if they thought about this stuff ahead of time, they'd still have jobs right now—and plenty of trees left."

Diamond snorted impatiently and Alex wheeled him around. Luther did the same with Sugar and they started back down the knoll.

"You should talk to my dad sometime," Alex said. "He goes on and on about this stuff. At least with the family."

"You seem to know a lot, too."

Alex shrugged. "I pick it up."

"It must be cool having a dad who works with wildlife."

"It is," said Alex, letting Diamond pick his way down the slope. "Especially when I was younger, he used to take me out in his truck all the time. We'd go to the game refuges and look for pronghorn and elk. Of course, there's a flip side."

"Like what?"

"Well, if someone gets mad at him for giving them a ticket or something, it's like my whole family has a big bull's-eye on it. Kind of like what's happening now."

"Your dad hasn't done anything."

Alex turned her head toward Luther. "No, but he's one of *them*. One of the *government people*. Since everyone's mad at the Forest Service, they're mad at my dad. And at me, too."

Luther thought about how he always saw Alex alone at school. "Not everyone feels that way."

"That's what I keep telling myself," she said. "But if there are people who don't, I haven't met them yet."

The trail narrowed and Alex pulled up. "Go ahead," she told Luther. Sugar scooted in front, and Luther's mind drifted back to the Forest Service meeting. Alex asked him something, but he only heard the last few words.

"Huh?" he asked, turning around in the saddle.

"I asked whether your family ever took any trips or anything. You know, away from Heartwood?"

"Uh, I've got an uncle down in San Jose."

"California?"

"Yeah. We've visited him a couple of times."

"Did you like it?"

"Yeah."

Alex laughed. "You sound real excited about it."

Luther looked back at her. "Sorry, I was thinking about something."

"Which was…?"

"That meeting last night. I was thinking maybe people feel the way they do around here because they don't have the right information. I mean, like, the newspaper this morning didn't really talk about the fires. It just talked about how mad everyone is."

"It's funny you should mention that."

"Why?"

"Well, I was kind of thinking the same thing—and that someone should do something about it."

"Yeah, someone should," Luther said, facing forward again.

"Luther, what I mean is that *we* should do something about it."

His head whipped back around. "Yeah right. We'll chain ourselves to a tree—like all the crazies in California and Oregon."

Alex shot him a sour look. "I'm serious, Luther. We could set up a table or something."

"A table?"

"Sure. You know how the Glee Club and ROTC and all those other groups have meetings at lunch?"

"Yeah."

"Well, we could have our own meetings."

"I think you have to be an official organization to do that," Luther said.

"So, we can start one."

"Hmmm...I don't think so," he said as Sugar again entered the willows.

"Come on, Luther. We could get information together and pass it out to the other students. Maybe we could even put together some events. It might be fun."

Fun wasn't exactly the word Luther had in mind. "I don't know. Maybe you should look for someone else to help you."

"Luther, there *is* no one else. You're perfect for this."

"Why?"

"Well, you obviously care about the issue. Also, you're a local. People know you and won't think it's just some outside agitator coming in to stir up trouble. If it were just me, people would be suspicious."

"Oh, I get it," Luther said, a touch of irritation in his voice. "So you just want to use me to push your own view-points? Is that why you invited me to ride today?"

Alex's mouth hung open for a moment, her face turning red. "Is *that* what you think?"

Luther knew he'd said the wrong thing, but he didn't like how she was pushing him. Instead of apologizing, he said, "How would I know? I only met you the other day. Maybe you *are* one of those radicals who just want to shut everything down so the bunnies and Bambi can play."

"Do I look like a radical to you?" Alex said, her voice rising.

"I don't know. I've never seen one up close before."

"Well, I'm not! I'm just using common sense!"

"Oh, and you're the only one with common sense around here?"

"That's not what I said at all. Jeez, you're just as bad as those people at the meeting last night," Alex said. "Are your ears plugged up or something?"

He stared at her. "I can hear just fine. Maybe it's you who don't know how to say anything."

Alex stared back at him, hurt scrawled across her face. "Just forget I brought it up."

Eight

When Luther got home, Roadkill nipped happily at his heels. Luther was in no mood to play. "No game," he said firmly as he stomped into the house.

He found his mom drinking coffee at the kitchen table, a health magazine open in front of her. "Oh, hi, Luther. I heated up some venison stew for dinner," she said, gesturing toward the stove. "It's a good thing deer season opens soon. That was the last venison in the freezer, so you'd better eat up."

"Thanks," Luther muttered, the conversation with Alex gnawing at him.

He reached into the cupboard for a bowl and ladled some stew out of the pot. Then he poured himself a glass of milk and sat down with his dinner across from his mom. He loved venison, but the stew felt tasteless in his mouth. *Why did I have to be such an idiot to Alex? What is it about her that sets me off like that?*

"Where've you been?" asked his mom. "I thought you'd be at the game."

"I'm not going. I went out riding instead."

"Bicycles?"

"Horses."

His mom looked surprised. "Who do you know who rides horses?"

"Just someone I met at school," he answered, shoving another bite of meat into his mouth.

"A girl?" his mom asked.

Luther swallowed and took a swig of milk. "Just a friend. Any word from Vic?"

"Actually, his crew finished mopping up a spot fire and he came home for the night."

Luther felt relieved. Maybe seeing Vic down by that creek wasn't so weird after all. If his stepfather got off work early, maybe he was just stopping with a friend to scope out a hunting blind or something. As his mom had pointed out, deer season lay just around the corner.

"Where is he?"

"At the game." She seemed to hesitate for a moment. "He promised Brenda he'd come watch her new cheer-leading routines."

Luther nodded, but his moment of relief turned to sadness. Last year, Vic had come to the games to watch *him* play.

His mom seemed to notice his mood shift. "Hey, I've got to run down to the Quik Mart," she said. "Give me some company."

"I don't know. I've got stuff to do."

"Come on, you've got the whole weekend, and I don't feel like sitting here cooped up in the house. You can drive. It's not that long until you'll be taking your driver's test." The opportunity to practice driving melted his resistance. After scraping the last of the stew from the bowl, Luther followed his mother outside with Roadkill trailing behind. As they approached his mom's small white car, she tossed him the keys.

"Can Roadkill come?" Luther asked.

"Why not?" Roadkill didn't wait for an invitation. As soon as the door opened, the Border collie leaped in.

His mother laughed. "It's not like we could stop him, is it?"

Luther shook his head and smiled despite his bad mood. No matter how low he felt, the Border collie always found some way to lift his spirits.

Luther climbed into the driver's seat, buckled up, and started the car. The engine rattled for a moment and then settled down. He steered out to the old highway and turned left into town. At the Quik Mart, he waited while his mother bought what she needed. After she climbed back into the passenger seat, Luther headed toward their house. Before they reached the turnoff, his mom said, "Why don't you keep driving? I don't feel like going home just yet."

As long as he was getting to drive, Luther decided to play along. "Where should we go?"

"I don't care," his mother said. "How about Ambush Point? I love the view from up there."

"Okay," Luther said hesitantly. Ambush Point did have a great view, but it also was the number one make-out spot in Heartwood—not a place you wanted to encourage your parents to visit.

Seeing Luther's doubtful face, his mother laughed. "Don't worry. I won't spy on anyone. Besides, while the game is on, there shouldn't be anyone up there, right?"

"I guess not."

"Okay then. Let's go."

A half-mile later, he flicked on the left blinker and turned onto a dirt and gravel road that headed up a mountainside. The tiny car wasn't a four-wheel drive, and the tires spun once or twice, kicking up clouds of dust behind them. Soon enough, though, they pulled into a large, flat clearing littered with beer bottles, cans, and other trash. One car was already parked to the side, and Luther gave it a wide berth.

After he turned off the engine, his mother rolled down her window and exclaimed, "No wonder you kids like to come up here!"

"Mom, keep your voice down!"

His mother's hand flew to her mouth. "Oh, right," she said, barely concealing a laugh. "I don't want to ruin your reputation!"

But Luther's mom was right. Below, a breathtaking scene greeted them. By now, the sun had disappeared behind the pall of smoke that filled the valley, and the lights of the town burned brightly. Just to the west of town, he could see the huge, hazy outline of the Apple Mountain mill poised next to the dark curves of the Clark Fork River. Surrounding the mill, acres of stacked logs waited to be processed.

Back toward them, Luther picked out different streets and buildings of the small downtown area. Closer still, he made out Heartwood High School and, next to it, the football stadium glowing under blazing blue-white floodlights. Even from up here, he could see the tiny forms of the cheerleaders whipping the packed crowd into a frenzy. He cracked his window. The deep pounding of drumbeats and wail of brass instruments from the band sent a burst of adrenaline surging through him.

"Sorry you're not down there?" his mother asked.

At that very moment, Luther would have given anything to be in the locker room with his friends suiting up for the game. But he shrugged and said, "Not really. It's all kind of stupid."

His mother nodded. They continued gazing down at the lights, and Roadkill squeezed up between the front seats. Luther wrapped his arm around the dog. Far below, the teams rushed out onto the stadium field, and the crowd roared. After a brief warm-up, two players from each team jogged to the center of the field for the coin toss. Luther wondered if Chet was one of them. He scanned the distant packed bleachers, also wondering where Vic was sitting.

His mother seemed to read his mind. "Don't worry about your stepfather," she said. "He's just having a hard time right now. Everything's changing with the work slowdown and you kids growing up. He thought things would be...different."

I'll bet you did, too, Luther thought, glancing over at his mom. He honestly couldn't see why she and Vic stayed together sometimes. There were so few times when they really seemed happy. Then again, maybe this life looked good compared to the life she'd had with his real father.

"Are you disappointed with me?" Luther suddenly asked.

The question seemed to catch his mom off guard, and her brown eyes swung toward him.

"Luther," she said, choosing her words carefully, "I don't always understand what you're going through, but you're a good boy—I mean, a good young man. I know things haven't been easy, but I'm confident you'll make decisions that are right for you."

His mom glanced back down at the stadium lights. "You know, you're probably right," she said. "Maybe this whole football and sports thing is stupid—at least for you. But for a lot of the kids around here, this may be the best part of their lives—the last time they can feel young and carefree and excited."

"That's a depressing thought," Luther said, absently gripping and regripping the steering wheel with his right hand.

"Maybe. But that's how it is a lot of times. Not everyone gets a chance to go out and make something more of their lives. That's why I'm glad you're working with Kay."

"You are?" Luther's head snapped toward her. He'd never heard her say anything like that before.

She nodded. "At first, I wasn't sure, but I can already see what it's done for you."

"What do you mean?"

"Well, before, you were just going with the flow. It didn't seem you had much of a plan or anything. Now, you're getting your own ideas about things and what you want your life to be. I can tell that you want to make a difference. I…I wish I'd met someone like Kay when I was your age."

Luther stared at his mom in astonishment. In the dim light coming through the windshield, he could see regret etched into her face. Then, he returned his gaze to the town and stadium below. Instead of focusing on the two teams crashing into each other, however, Luther's mind drifted back to Alex and their earlier conversation.

Before going to Kay's the next morning, Luther detoured through town and stopped by the hardware store. As usual on the morning after a game, Heartwood looked like a ghost town, and Luther appreciated not having to worry about traffic. He parked his bike in front of the store and walked in to find Mr. Ingold, the owner, standing next to the front register.

"Morning, Luther. Help you find something?"

"Just picking up a round file."

"You know where they are?"

Luther nodded.

"Your timing's good. We had a run on them because of all the fires, but I got another shipment in yesterday."

"Great. Thanks."

Wandering back into the aisles, Luther quickly found the file section. He examined a couple of sizes, finally selecting one he thought would do the job. As he headed back toward the front of the store, he almost collided with a customer carrying two large gas cans.

"Oh, sorry," Luther said.

The man grunted and barely glanced his way, but Luther immediately recognized him. It was the man he'd seen talking to Vic the previous afternoon. After the customer paid for the gas cans and left, Luther walked to the counter.

"Sharpening some chainsaws today?" Mr. Ingold asked, ringing up the file.

"Just one," Luther said. "Uh, Mr. Ingold, do you know that man who just left?"

The storeowner laughed and glanced at the door, though the man was long gone. "Sure. I know everybody around here. That's Clifton Hanks."

Clifton Hanks. That's right, Luther thought, dredging the name from his memory.

"Used to work over at the mill," Mr. Ingold explained. "Like a lot of others, he got cut last year."

"You don't know if he's working as a firefighter, do you?"

The older man ran his hand thoughtfully through his gray hair. "I think he is. That's the only way he and a lot of other folks are scraping by these days, you know. Why do you ask?"

"Just curious. Thanks."

Nine

After a quick stop back home to collect Roadkill, Luther pedaled out to Kay's. His chest felt like it was filled with Super Balls as he drove his legs fiercely into each stroke of the pedals. *What was Clifton Hanks doing buying gasoline cans?* Most people in Heartwood kept gas cans to fill up chainsaws or, in the winter, snowmobiles, but what were the odds Hanks would need new ones today—right after Luther had over-heard him talking with Vic? *Is there a connection? Could Vic really have something to do with these fires?*

He wondered if he should ask Kay what she thought, but when he got to her place, Godzilla was gone, and Luther's bird chores quickly pushed Vic to the back of his mind.

But that didn't mean he'd forgotten about the fires. As soon as he finished feeding the birds, Luther took down Kay's old chainsaw from the back porch. He set it on the ground and anchored it by sliding his foot through the wraparound handle. Then, with the new round file in hand, he began carefully sharpening the cutting edges of the chain.

It took him about twenty minutes to get the chain the way he wanted it, but he enjoyed the work. One of many things he'd learned from Vic was to take pleasure in keeping equipment in top shape. Luther planned to replace the spark plug, top off the chain oil, and clean the filter. As he was testing the last of the saw's sharp cutting edges, however, he heard Godzilla rumble up in front of the house, so he returned the chainsaw to its hook on the wall.

Walking around to the front of the house, he saw Kay removing a brown paper bag from the passenger side of the truck.

"Hi," Luther said.

Kay started. "Oh, Luther, I didn't know you were here. Where's Roadkill?"

"He's probably checking out some bear scat or something down by the river. I didn't think you'd be back so early."

"Neither did I," Kay said, her voice drained of its usual cheerfulness. "Someone gave me this and I thought I ought to get it into the freezer."

She handed Luther the brown paper bag, and even before he looked inside, his heart sank with the knowledge of what it held. He wasn't wrong.

Inside the bag lay the bloodied body of a small raptor. "A kestrel?"

"Yep," Kay said, her lips pressed tightly together. "He was probably sitting there on a telephone pole or a fence waiting for a juicy butterfly to come along, and someone just drove up and blew him away."

Luther had never heard Kay sound so bitter.

She ran her hand absently through her wild hair. "I just don't get it, Luther. I thought we were making progress around here, that we were out of the Dark Ages and people were starting to appreciate raptors. Then, *bam!* dead birds are showing up like it was the 1940s or '50s again, when the only good raptor was a dead raptor. What's gone wrong?"

Luther just shook his head.

"I mean, what else can I do?" Kay continued. "I give education programs at the schools. I talk to people about these birds all the time and let them see how cool they are up close. What am I missing?"

Luther's mind flashed back to the Forest Service meeting two nights earlier—especially the crowd's anger and the tension when Knot Juddson and his cronies stormed out of the high school gym. "People are mad right now," he told Kay. "Maybe some of them are taking it out on the birds."

Kay looked at him, pain creasing her face. "But it doesn't make sense! Am I doing something wrong?"

"You're not doing anything wrong," Luther told her.

You just can't do it all by yourself.

When they returned home, Roadkill raced into the house and barked a greeting to Brenda. At the same time, Luther accidentally slammed the front door behind him.

"Too loud!" Brenda groaned. Though it was almost noon, she still slumped on the couch in her bathrobe, staring vacantly at the television screen. She hardly glanced at Luther, but said in an accusing voice, "Why are you up so early?"

"Rough night partying?"

"It was a *good* night partying. It's this morning that isn't so great."

"You'll live," Luther told her without sympathy and walked into the kitchen. He made himself a ham-and-cheese sandwich and dumped a small mountain of tortilla chips beside it on the plate. He carried his lunch out to the living room and sat on the couch next to his sister.

Brenda scowled at him as he bit off a huge hunk of the sandwich.

"Want some?" he asked.

Brenda blocked the sight of the sandwich with her hand. "Ugh. You're going to make me sick." After a minute she grumbled, "You missed a good game last night. We killed 'em."

"How'd Chet do?"

"Awesome. You would've, too. You should go out again next year. The girls would be all over you."

"I don't think so."

Brenda shrugged. "Can't say I didn't try."

After obliterating the mound of tortilla chips, Luther walked back into the kitchen, rinsed off his plate, and picked up the new phone book. Before opening it, he had to think for a moment. Then he flipped the pages to the M's, found the number he was looking for, and dialed.

He was surprised when Alex answered. "Oh, hi," he said lamely.

"Luther?"

"I, uh, thought you'd be out at the stables."

"No, not today." Alex's voice sounded cold. Distant.

Luther wrapped the phone cord around his fingers. "Oh."

An awkward silence filled the phone line before Alex said, "So, did you just feel like playing with the phone buttons or is there another reason you called?"

"Well, I was thinking—"

"I hope you didn't hurt yourself."

He sighed. She wasn't making this any easier.

"No," he said. "I mean about the idea we were talking about."

More silence.

"The idea to start a new student group," he continued. "I've been thinking that maybe we should go ahead and do it."

Luther listened to his own breathing as he waited for a reply. Finally, Alex asked, "What changed your mind?"

With Kay and the dead kestrel fresh in his brain, Luther remembered what his mom had said the night before about making a difference. "I'm not sure," he told Alex, twisting the phone cord around his finger until his fingertip turned purple. "Maybe I realized I'd regret it if I didn't try to do something to help around here."

"You mean guilt drove you to it?" Alex asked, her voice lighter.

Luther gave a half-snort. "Yeah. Maybe."

"Well, that works for me."

"But," Luther said, "I don't want our group to be just about the fires and the forest. I want it to be about wildlife, too."

Alex went silent again for a moment. Then, to Luther's surprise, she said, "I think that's a good idea. It'll tie everything together."

"Okay."

"Okay."

That afternoon, Luther rode over to Kay's and asked her some questions about raptors and their role in the forest ecosystem. Afterward, he went to the Heartwood Public Library and began looking up more information on fires, logging, and government policy. Though Luther had done some research the week before, he asked Ms. Gonzales the head librarian for help. She directed him to some magazines and websites he'd never heard of.

As he pored over the information, he realized that there was a lot more to fire and forest issues than he'd ever understood. Apple Mountain Timber Company and much of the town blamed the government for protecting certain stands of old-growth forests. Everyone knew that. Yet Luther quickly discovered that the vast majority of logs for Apple Mountain—and for most lumber companies—

came from private lands, *not* public forests. "So," Luther asked himself, "why is everyone so mad at the government for closing some of the national forests to logging?"

After about an hour, Luther found at least part of the answer on a website that had been created by several former Apple Mountain employees. They had been fired for disagreeing with the company's timber management policies and had created the website to educate the public about what was really going on. According to them, Apple Mountain had been bought by a large multinational company several years before—something Luther remembered Vic talking about. What Luther *hadn't* heard was that from the beginning, the new company had no intention of managing the forests responsibly. Instead, it began "liquidating"—cutting down—their forests as fast as possible for maximum profit.

"So that's what's going on," Luther muttered under his breath. He'd been vaguely aware that the pace of Apple Mountain's operations had increased when the new owners took over but it had never registered with him why. The more he read, the more things began to crystallize.

According to the website, instead of trying to preserve a long-term forest industry, the company's plan was to sell off all the usable trees and then market the land for vacation homes, ski areas, and other real estate ventures. With tourists and home-seekers flocking to Montana, Apple Mountain could make far more money in real estate than it could in logging.

The owners of the company don't really believe the government is causing their problems, Luther realized.

They're just trying to make everyone else think that to distract them from what's really happening.

Either way, Apple Mountain came out on top. If the logging restrictions stayed in place, no one would blame Apple Mountain for shutting down the mill. On the other hand, if they somehow managed to get the logging restrictions overturned, the company would get more cheap logs from the national forests—and reap even greater profits.

Luther realized that the company's stance on the fires was just part of the whole diversion. Blaming the fires on the government's logging restrictions was simply one more way to keep people from looking at what Apple Mountain was doing to its own forests.

The next morning, Luther typed up information describing how Apple Mountain was mismanaging its forests and how that was hurting the entire Montana forest products industry. He also put together a flyer on birds of prey and another one listing the arguments for protecting certain areas from logging. Meanwhile, Alex focused on compiling a sheet on wildlife in general and the importance of wildfires to forest ecosystems.

On Monday, Luther and Alex stayed after their first period class to ask Mr. Gary if he would be the academic sponsor for their new organization.

"I'd be delighted," he told them. "What are you going to call it?"

"The Student Forest Society," Alex told him.

Mr. Gary nodded. "Not bad. Just be careful how you word things. As you know, you're dealing with some pretty explosive issues here."

"We know," Luther said.

At lunch Luther and Alex went to the vice principal's office to register their new organization.

"Student Forest Society?" Mrs. Donovan asked, looking at them over the rims of her glasses.

"Yes," Alex replied. "We thought with all that's going on, there should be a student group involved with the issues."

"May I see your flyers?"

Luther handed them to her and the vice principal read them over. After she finished, she sighed. "I don't think you're going to find much support, but I won't stop you from trying."

"Thank you," Alex said. "We were also wondering if we could set up a table this week to let students know about the group?"

Mrs. Donovan pursed her lips. "Well, that's not usually how groups get members."

"We know," Alex said, "but if we just put up signs for the meeting or add it to the morning announcements, students might not understand what we're doing."

"We thought setting up a table for a couple of days would let people know what we're about," Luther added.

"I'll give you three days," the vice principal said, "as long as it doesn't interfere with other school activities."

"Thank you," Alex said.

Leaving the office, Luther and Alex gave each other a high five.

"Well," said Luther. "I guess we're really going to do this."

"Yes. Today we set up a table," said Alex with just a touch of sarcasm, "tomorrow, we change the world."

Tuesday morning, Luther biked to school at his usual time. He'd skipped breakfast—too many nerves dancing through his stomach. Now that he and Alex were actually going to debut the SFS, doubts filled his head. *How will people react to our group? Will it make them angry? Or even worse, what if no one pays any attention at all?*

He didn't know the answers. He'd just come to the point that trying something was better than sitting around watching everything happen around him.

After he locked his bike to the rack, he saw Chet walking toward the school's main entrance. Luther took a deep breath.

"Hey, Chet," he called.

Chet wheeled stiffly, hands thrust into the deep pockets of his letterman jacket.

Luther approached him. "I, uh, heard you had a good game Friday night. Way to go."

Chet's face softened and he shrugged. "I did okay."

"Five unassisted tackles and a fumble recovery?" Luther said. "That's better than okay."

"Uh, thanks."

Chet turned and entered the front doors. Luther watched him and, after a moment, followed.

At lunch, Luther was first to reach the commons, an

outside area where, if temperatures were above ten or twenty below, most of the students hung out after eating. It was also where student groups often set up tables to promote various activities or events. A custodian had already set out a table for them, but Luther dragged it over a few feet so that it stood in the shade of a maple tree. A minute later, he spotted Alex walking toward him with a large cardboard tube.

"What's that? A hand-held missile launcher?"

"As a matter of fact, it is. So you'd better be nice to me." Alex set down her backpack and began pulling something out of the tube.

As she unrolled it, Luther read the banner's bold green and orange letters: "Student Forest Society." His face broke into a grin. "Hey, that's great!"

"I thought we could hang it in front of the table," Alex said. "We can also put it up when you chain yourself to a tree."

"Very funny."

Luther helped Alex tack up the banner. As they began setting out their flyers, Luther noticed passing kids eyeing them curiously. After Luther and Alex sat down, it wasn't long before a couple of students stopped to ask what they were doing. When Luther told them, they scrunched up their faces and said, "No thanks."

They didn't have any better luck with the next few kids who dropped by.

"That's okay," Alex said. "We're not going to change people's minds overnight."

"Yeah, but sometime this millennium would be nice."

A moment later, a girl from their homeroom approached. Luther recognized her as Eliza, the skinny girl who'd mentioned global warming in Current Topics the previous week.

"Hi," he said. "It's Eliza, right?"

Without bothering to answer, Eliza asked, "What's the Student Forest Society? What do you do?"

"Well," said Luther, clearing his throat. "We don't do much yet, but—"

"Allow *me*," Alex interrupted, giving Luther a shut-up-and-listen look. "We organized to help provide students with unbiased information about what's going on in the forests. We don't feel that the community of Heartwood is being told the complete story about the fires, logging, and other issues that affect us."

Luther handed the girl a flyer, and he and Alex waited while she read it all the way through. "You know," Eliza finally said, "I saw a show about this on TV last summer. It has been bothering me a lot. And ever since we started talking about this in class, I've realized that it doesn't seem like anyone really wants to hear the truth. They just want to believe what's easiest to believe."

Luther and Alex looked at each other with raised eyebrows.

"If you'd like to join SFS," Alex said, "we hope you'll come to our first meeting. Besides the forest issues, we also want to work on things that are affecting wildlife in the area."

"What do you do? I mean, you're not planning to go out there driving nails into logs so they'll break the mill's saws and stuff, are you?"

Alex laughed. "Not quite. But if you join us," she said, "you can help us decide what to do. We're meeting this Friday in Mr. Gary's room."

Eliza picked up the other flyer. "I'll think about it," she said. "Bye."

"See you later," said Alex.

After Eliza was out of earshot, Luther said, "Hey, why'd you interrupt me when I started telling her what we did?"

Alex rolled her eyes. "Because you weren't telling her what we did. You were telling her that we *didn't* do anything."

"I was not! I was just about to explain that we were just starting up and everything."

"And by the time you finished, lunch would've been over. Besides, you were so busy flirting, I doubt you'd have said anything intelligent."

Luther protested. "I was *not* flirting. How—?"

"Give me some credit," said Alex. "I can tell when a guy's got the hots for someone."

"The *hots?*"

Luther was about to object further when four football players approached their table. Out in front walked an all-too-familiar figure.

"What's this B.S.?" Warren Juddson snarled, towering over Alex and Luther.

"Warren Juddson," Alex said, in a sprightly voice. "Great to see you. We're here to help educate students just like you so you can make better decisions about the direction our community is going."

"*Our* community? You don't even belong here."

Luther opened his mouth to cut in, but Alex spoke first. "You're absolutely right. I'm still a newcomer, but I think you'll find this information helpful."

Alex handed Warren the flyers. Without even looking at them, he crumpled them in his fist and threw them to the ground. Then he planted his huge paws on the table and leaned over until his face hovered a foot from Luther's.

"I don't know what kind of crap you and your girlfriend think you're pulling, Wright, but you'd better watch it."

Adrenaline dumped into Luther's veins. "We're not 'pulling' anything," he said. "We have a right to be here. And watch who you're threatening."

Luther's muscles tensed, ready to spring into action, but at the last second, Warren straightened back up.

"It's not a threat," he said, staring at Luther. "It's a promise."

Warren paused a moment to let his words sink in, then turned and walked away. His cronies followed, growling and snickering among themselves. He was glad he couldn't hear what they were saying.

"Whew," Alex said. "Good thing I don't have asthma. Between the smoke and the testosterone in the air, I'd be dead for sure right now."

Luther tried to calm himself. "Moron," he said.

Alex looked at him. "I beg your pardon?"

"Not you. Him."

Alex waved her hand. "That jerk? His kind are a dime a dozen. All bark and no bite..."

Luther took a deep breath. A year ago, he would have readily agreed with Alex. After all, he'd known Warren for years and figured he could read him pretty well. But this wasn't last year. Now there was a new hostility, a new hardness in Warren's eyes. Luther knew it wasn't just about the logging or the fires. Some of it came from the playoff game with Dillon the previous November. Warren had played in that same game. More importantly, he and Luther had been at the same party afterward.

But instead of trying to explain, Luther just said, "Yeah. You're probably right."

Ten

efore the lunch period ended, several more students stopped by the table. A couple of boys from Luther's homeroom made snide remarks and tried to start up an argument, but most kids just glanced at the flyers and moved on quickly. One boy, a junior, stayed several minutes, asking serious questions about the fires, Apple Mountain, and logging.

As they rolled up their banner, Alex beamed. "That rocked. For a town like Heartwood, I'd score that an unqualified success."

Luther silently slid the banner back into its tube and replaced the plastic caps on the ends.

"Hey, what's wrong?" Alex asked. "You don't look happy."

He shrugged. "What good was all this? Most of the kids who came by seemed to resent us or at least what we were trying to tell them."

Alex rapped him lightly on the head. "Hello, Luther Wright. This is earth calling!"

Luther ducked away. "Huh? What?"

"All great social and political movements start this way. People are uncomfortable with new ideas. Do you think white America immediately embraced Martin Luther King Jr.? Or that the world believed Rachel Carson right away about toxic chemicals?"

"Who's Rachel Carson?"

Alex gave a huge mock sigh. "Oh, man. We've got to educate you. She's only the person who practically *started* the modern environmental movement. The point is, Luther, this is a great beginning. You should be happy about it."

As Luther collected the last of the flyers, he still wasn't convinced. "Maybe you're right."

"Of course I'm right. Anyway, I've got to head to biology. Talk to you later?"

"Yeah. Sure."

After the last bell, Luther stopped by his locker to drop off the books he didn't need for homework. Then he trotted down the school steps and walked toward the bike rack. A bunch of kids were milling around gawking at something, and Luther pushed his way through. On the ground, he saw the mangled remains of his ten-speed. Both wheels were bent with most of the spokes kicked in. The front derailleur lay smashed while the rear one had been twisted inward, obviously ruined. Both gear shifters had been snapped off and the seat was in shreds.

"What happened?" Luther asked, at first thinking there'd been some kind of freak accident. No one answered. Then it dawned on Luther that this wasn't an accident.

Alex elbowed her way through the crowd. "Luther, what happened?"

Luther didn't even look up.

"Who did this?"

One of the students standing around said, "We didn't see it happen. It was like this when we got here."

"God, what a mess," Alex said to Luther. "You okay?"

"Yeah." But he didn't feel okay. Heat was building degree by degree inside him. "It's a warning," he muttered.

Alex looked at him. "What?"

"They're warning me to stop doing the table and asking questions."

"Who is?"

The onlookers unlocked their own bikes and began drifting away.

Luther let out an angry snort. "Take your pick."

Alex lowered her voice. "You think Warren did it?"

"Maybe," he said. "But it could have been anyone."

"I never thought they'd do something like this."

"I should have expected it."

"Well, come on. Let's go to the principal's office and call the police. We can file a report. Maybe they can find out who did it."

"You don't get it, Alex. The police aren't going to do anything. They might even be parents of the kids who did this."

Luther angrily kicked at the bike's ruined back tire, and they both stared at the wreck. Finally, Alex said, "Maybe I was wrong about SFS. Maybe we should just scrap the idea. I mean, if they'd do this, who knows what else they might do?"

"No."

Alex looked at him. "No? No what?"

"They want us to quit. To run away."

"Come on, Luther. It's not about running away. It's about common sense."

"No. You were right the first time. I'm not going to let them get to me."

After a moment Alex said, "Well, I've got my dad's truck. Let me at least give you a ride out to Kay's."

"Okay. Thanks." Luther unlocked his bike's carcass and hoisted it over his shoulder.

"Jeez." Alex couldn't hold back a chuckle. "They really did a number on it, didn't they?"

Luther managed a weak grin, but the steel cords in his stomach twisted tighter. "Yeah. They totaled it."

Alex led the way to a large blue pickup and unlocked the doors. Luther dropped the bike in the truck bed and walked around to the passenger side.

Settling onto the comfortable bench seat, he asked, "When did you get your license?"

Alex closed the door after her. "My birthday, in August. You working on yours?"

"My birthday's in January. I want to get my license *that day.*"

Alex smiled and started the truck. "It comes in handy."

"This is nice," Luther said, running his hand over the truck's soft seat covers.

"My dad got it a couple years ago. Fish and Wildlife jobs don't pay much, but they're steadier than working for Apple Mountain."

"I guess they would be. I'd like to get one of these some day."

"You will—as long as you get out of Heartwood," Alex said, pulling out of the school parking lot.

"Yeah… You mind if we stop by my house first? I want to drop off my bike and change my clothes."

"No problem."

Alex shifted the truck into a higher gear and followed Luther's directions to his house. When they arrived, Brenda and Sam stood talking next to Sam's red Neon. They turned to stare as the blue pickup rolled up next to them. Roadkill ran in from across the field and began barking.

"Oh man, I thought Brad Pitt was pulling up," Sam quipped as Luther hopped out the passenger side. "Nice truck."

"It's not mine," Luther said, bending over to rub his dog's chest.

"Oh, *really,*" Brenda said. "I thought maybe you got your big bonus from Kay today. Who's your friend?"

"Alex, this is my sister Brenda. That's Sam."

"Hi," Alex said.

Brenda inspected Alex. "I've seen you at school, haven't I?"

"We're in Spanish together."

"Luther," Sam said. "Why've you been holding out on us? No one told us you had a girlfriend."

Alex laughed.

Luther turned the color of a wild strawberry. "We're not... Uh, she's not..."

"Oh, I see," said Sam. "Still playin' it cool, huh?"

Luther lifted the remains of his bike out of the truck bed.

"Jesus!" said Sam. "What ran over you?"

"I knew this forest society thing was a bad idea." Brenda walked over to the bike, shaking her head. "What's the matter with you? I thought you were my smart little brother?"

Luther brushed past her and dropped the bike with a crash onto the cement of the garage floor.

"Dad's going to flip about this. You know that, don't you?" Brenda called to him.

"I'll be out in a minute," he told Alex. He and Roadkill walked into the house, where Luther dumped his stuff and changed into his work clothes. When he came out, Sam had left. Brenda and Alex were still talking.

"You ready?" Luther asked Alex.

"Boy, little brother, you really know how to dress up for a girl," Brenda said.

Alex again laughed. Luther hadn't even thought about how bad his "bird-poop" clothes looked.

"That's okay," said Alex. "My work clothes look almost as bad."

"Let's go," Luther said.

"Hey, don't be in such a rush," said Brenda. "I like your friend here. She's got more sense than you do."

"You mind if Roadkill rides in back?" Luther asked Alex, ignoring his sister.

"He can ride in front with us," she said. "I like dogs."

"Great." Luther opened the passenger door, and Roadkill hopped up onto the bench seat. Turning to Brenda, Luther said, "Tell Mom I'll be home at the usual time."

"Tell her yourself," Brenda said. "I'll be out of here. By the way, did you hear about the new fires?"

Luther's hand froze on the door. "What new fires?"

"There's a big one in the mountains behind Demming, about ten miles east of here. Just flared up. Dad'll be home tonight, but they're sending him there first thing in the morning."

Luther stared at his sister, his mouth open.

"What's the matter?" Brenda asked. "The fire's too far away for us to worry about."

"It's…nothing," Luther mumbled. But his mind had already turned to Vic, Clifton Hanks, and the gas cans.

"Bye," Alex said, walking around the truck to the driver's side.

"Nice meeting you," said Brenda. "Keep him in line."

Alex smiled as she got in and turned the key in the ignition. She put the truck in reverse and backed around, then wheeled onto the road.

"Brenda seems nice," Alex said.

Luther shrugged. "She's my stepsister. She thinks she knows everything."

"That's just the way we big sisters are. It's because we *do* know everything."

Luther's mind was swirling. What if his stepfather had started the Demming fire? What if Vic really was involved? For Luther, thoughts that had been an abstract fantasy suddenly turned frighteningly real.

After a moment, he realized Alex had asked him a question. He refocused. "What? Um, sorry. I was just thinking."

"Thinking *again?*" Alex teased. "What was it this time?"

"Uh, nothing… Did you say you have brothers and sisters?" Luther asked, forcing away thoughts of Vic and the new fire.

"A brother in middle school, but he's even a bigger pain than you are, so I don't let him out much."

Luther scratched Roadkill under the chest. The dog stood with his paws on the dash, peering intently out the front window. "He loves going for rides."

"He's beautiful. Where'd you get him?"

"I was walking home from school a couple winters ago when I spotted him next to the road. It looked like someone had just abandoned him out there—no tags or anything—so I brought him home."

"I'm afraid to ask how he got the name Roadkill."

Luther laughed. "When I found him, he was gnawing on the frozen carcass of a deer that had been hit, so I decided that would be his name. He's a smart dog. He learned it pretty fast."

"Remind me not to let you name any of *my* pets," Alex told him.

Luther pointed toward the turnoff. "This is it, right up here."

Alex downshifted and turned into Kay's place.

Luther noticed that Godzilla was missing from the drive.

"Doesn't look like anyone's here," Alex said.

"No. Kay's been really busy the last few weeks." Luther opened the passenger door and Roadkill hopped over him to the ground.

"It must be really great working with the birds," Alex said. "I'd love to see them sometime."

Luther paused a moment. "You want to see them now?"

Alex frowned. "I can't today. It's my turn to shovel out the stalls at the stables. How about tomorrow?"

Luther shrugged. "Sure. See you then."

"Okay." Alex turned the truck around and waved out the window.

"Thanks for the ride!" Luther shouted.

After watching Alex drive off, Luther called Roadkill, who was sniffing at something near a sage bush—probably something rotten, Luther guessed.

"Well," he asked as the dog trotted toward him, "where should we start?"

Luther decided to feed the eagles their rabbits first. Then he went to Hawk Heaven, and after that the owl house. As he gave the owls the last of their mice, Luther heard Kay pull up out front. By the time he closed the shed door behind him, he saw Kay walking over from the house.

His boss seemed to have recovered her positive attitude since finding the dead kestrel the week before. "Hey, Luth!" she shouted. "How's my favorite face? I didn't think you were here, but then I saw Roadkill. Where's your bike?"

"It had an, uh, accident."

Luther told Kay about the bike and his first day setting up the Student Forest Society table. Kay listened, then clapped her hands together. "Luther, that's great!"

Luther looked at her like she was crazy. "Great? Which part? Getting abused by everyone who came by the table or having my bike destroyed?"

"Don't you see? You're getting their attention."

"It's not the *kind* of attention I was looking for."

Kay grinned and slapped him on the back. "Maybe not. But give it some time. I'm really proud of you. You're not just standing around griping. You're *doing* something."

Luther was still doubtful, but Kay's words felt good. As they walked toward the falcon house, Kay asked, "You all done with the birds?"

"Just have the falcons to go," Luther said.

"Great. I've got some time for flying. You in?"

Roadkill jumped and hopped around them. The dog definitely wanted in.

"Kay, I was wondering," Luther said. "I got all this information about fires and stuff from the Forest Service. One pamphlet recommended clearing all the vegetation within fifty feet of any buildings. Do you want me to tackle some of that brush?"

Kay stopped and they examined the farm grounds. Knapweed, tansy, and sage covered most of the area, and in some places reached right up to the buildings. The ponderosa pine next to Kay's house worried Luther the most.

It was small as pines went—only about forty feet high—but its lower branches scraped the top of Kay's wood-shingled roof. If a fire came near that tree, they might as well just set a match to the place and walk away.

Kay sighed. "I've been thinking about that, too. If anything happened to the birds or my artwork, I don't know what I'd do."

"I wouldn't mind getting started now," Luther told her.

Kay hesitated, then relented. "Okay. Sal can wait. Let's start with the smaller stuff around the bird houses. Then this weekend, I can borrow a tractor or something to drag the larger areas between the buildings and around the house."

"Sounds good."

While Luther finished feeding the falcons, Kay walked to her back porch and grabbed a hoe, a shovel, and a Pulaski—a half-axe, half-hoe tool used by firefighters. Together, she and Luther worked hard, digging out weeds and hacking down sage bushes, but the work went more slowly than Luther had expected. It took them more than an hour just to clear a small strip around the falcon house.

"Whew, this is tougher than I thought it'd be," Kay said, stopping for a break. She took a drink from a bottle of water and then handed it to Luther.

"We've still got a couple hours of light," he said. "We can probably clear an area around Hawk Heaven, too."

Kay looked over the grounds. "Maybe, but I'm thinking it doesn't make sense for us to hack and chop like this when we could get it all done with a tractor in fifteen or twenty minutes. Let's knock off for today. I'll get a tractor lined up for this weekend, and we'll do it right."

Luther was too tired to object. "You're the boss," he said.

Eleven

uther was sitting at his desk doing homework when he heard Vic's truck pull up. His stepfather opened the front door, then slammed it shut behind him.

"Where is he?" Vic yelled, his voice shaking the house.

"Vic, don't—" Luther heard his mother say.

A second later, his stepfather burst into his room. Luther spun around and stood up. Black soot covered Vic's clothes and face, and he still wore the safety helmet over his matted hair. His eyes burned like coals.

"What the hell do you think you're doing?" he demanded.

A chill ran down Luther's spine and he tried to speak. "Wha—?"

"This student forest crap!" His stepfather held up one of the flyers Luther and Alex had put together and shook it in his face. "Do you want us to go on welfare? Just who the hell do you think you are?"

Luther backed up against his desk.

"Vic, stop it!" his mother said, appearing in the doorway.

"I'm talking to Luther! Answer me!"

Luther swallowed. "I just thought...people needed to know the truth."

"Truth!" his stepfather yelled, enraged. "Whose truth? The Sierra Club's? The liberal bureaucrats?"

"N-no. About the fires and Apple Mountain."

His stepfather's voice became cold and hard. "I'll tell you the truth. If I can't go out there and cut logs for the mill, we've got nothing. We *need* those logs the government has locked up out there, you understand that? They've got us between a rock and a hard place. They won't let us cut the trees, and now they're letting the fires burn up the timber. The only way we can get a paycheck at all is to watch our futures burn up in front of us! How is *that* for some truth!"

Luther looked down at the floor.

"You getting any of this?" Vic demanded.

Numb, Luther remained silent.

His stepfather moved closer until Luther could feel his hot breath on his face. "I want you to tell me you're going to knock this crap off, do you hear me?"

Luther tried to speak, but his voice wouldn't respond.

"I said, do you hear me?" his stepfather repeated, louder.

Time stopped as Luther raised his eyes and stared at his stepfather. Vic glared back.

"Okay," Vic growled. "Have it your way." He wheeled around and stomped out of the room, brushing past his wife.

Luther's mother glanced after his stepfather and then

looked back at her son, the apology in her eyes. "Are you okay? Want me to bring you something to eat?"

Luther barely nodded as she left the room.

❧

Walking to school the next morning, Luther still felt rattled, like he'd been beaten up. He couldn't remember ever seeing Vic so angry. He'd known his stepfather would disapprove if he ever saw the flyers, but the violent outburst had caught Luther off guard. His insides churned, and he couldn't stop wondering if all this might have something to do with the new fire. Was Vic involved?

As he neared the high school, he spotted Alex sitting on the wall in front. She waved as he approached.

"There you are," she said. "I wasn't sure how you were going to get here. My dad had to use his truck or I—" Alex stopped in mid-sentence. "What's wrong, Luther? Are you sick?"

He sat down next to her.

"I got into it with my stepdad last night. I mean, he got into it with me."

"What happened?"

Luther began telling her about it and Alex let him talk. After he'd finished, she said, "That must have been hard."

Luther took a deep breath. "He's never gone off on me that bad before."

"What are you going to do?"

"I've been asking myself that... Listen, Alex. Can I tell you something else?"

"Sure."

Luther recounted the conversation he'd overheard between Vic and Clifton Hanks. The five-minute bell rang, and students started filing into the school, but Luther kept talking. He also told Alex about running into Clifton at the hardware store and about Vic's comments about the fires. When he finished, he looked at Alex. "Am I just imagining things or do you think Vic is involved in this somehow?"

Alex gave a low whistle. "Jeez, Luther. I haven't even met your stepfather. You said he was against poaching. Is he the kind of person who would go out and light forest fires just to have a job?"

Luther didn't used to think so, but now… His anger from the night before resurfaced. Why had Vic yelled at him like that?

"Who knows?" Luther said. "He and my mom have been scrambling to get by for a long time."

"But you're talking about *arson,*" Alex said, keeping her voice low. "In a place like Montana, that's almost like talking about killing babies or something."

"I know."

The next bell rang.

"We're late again," Luther said.

Alex nodded. "Maybe you should sit on this for a while. At least until you find more evidence. I mean, what you said sort of makes sense, but this is serious. Real serious. And you don't have any solid proof, do you?"

"No," he admitted.

Alex absently hooked her finger under her leather necklace. "Do what you think is right, Luther, but if I were you, I wouldn't say anything yet. Try giving it a few days and see if you find out anything more."

He nodded.

They both stood up. Alex adjusted her backpack over her shoulder and asked, "Luther, do you still want to do the table? I mean, I'll understand if you want to give it up, at least for now."

"No, I want to do it," he said, with more defiance than he'd intended.

Alex stared back. "Are you sure? You've got a lot more at stake than I do."

He ran it quickly through his brain. "Yeah, I'm sure.

Overnight, word had gotten out about SFS. At lunch, Luther and Alex found several kids waiting for them when they arrived at the table. By the time they tacked up their banner and sat down, more than a dozen of their class-mates had gathered around. Most of them jeered or made sarcastic comments, but to Luther's amazement, several kids stood up for them and traded barbs with the hecklers. Three students even signed up to join the group.

"This is amazing," whispered Alex. "Can you believe this?"

Luther shook his head. "No." But even in the midst of the commotion, his mind kept darting back to the new fire and his confrontation with Vic the night before.

Just then, Mr. Gary cleared a path to the table. "How's it going?" he asked.

"Pretty good," said Luther.

Mr. Gary glanced at the kids milling around. "Yes, I can see. Any problems?"

Luther shook his head. "No. Not really."

"Just having a spirited debate," Alex added.

Mr. Gary chuckled. "Well, let me know."

"We will."

Luther and Alex continued to answer questions, address comments, and hand out flyers until the last few students tired of trading insults or drifted away to eat. Luther took a deep breath. "Wow," he said.

"You can say that again. We're out of flyers."

"I'll bet we find most of them in the garbage can."

Alex punched him in the shoulder. "Quit being so cynical. A lot of people will read them."

Luther shrugged. "Maybe a few. You hungry?"

Before Alex could answer, Warren Juddson and his buddies lumbered up to the table. "You still here?" Warren demanded.

Emboldened by the turnout at lunch, Luther stood. "Yeah, I'm here, but you'd better get going. I hear the mill needs some two-by-fours, and your head's probably the right thickness."

A couple of the football players stifled laughs. Warren glared at Luther and then at Alex.

"Did you read the flyer?" Alex asked.

Warren's face twisted as he spoke. "I thought you could take a hint," he growled. "But you're dumber than I thought."

"Well, you're the expert on dumbness around here,"

Luther said, knowing he should keep his mouth shut.

"You think you're better than everyone else, don't you?" Warren put his hands on the table and leaned toward Luther. "Well, me and you both know that's not true. The only difference between me and you," he hissed, "is I stick with my friends." Warren whirled around and stomped off.

"Our first club meeting is next week," Alex called after him. "Come on by."

Luther just stared after Warren. When he disappeared, Alex asked, "He's the one who smashed up your bike, isn't he?"

"Probably."

"I shouldn't have said what I did. It might make him do something even worse."

Luther shrugged, but it wasn't Alex's joke that bothered him. It was Warren's comment about sticking with his friends. "Don't worry about it, Alex. He's just messed up."

But Luther knew as well as Warren that an ugly truth hovered between them.

As they rolled up their banner, Luther tried to shake Warren from his brain. "So, you still want to see the birds today?" he asked Alex. "I think Kay will be there and you can meet her, too."

"Sure. Do I need to bring anything special?"

"You got a car?"

"I can get one. My mom'll probably let me take hers. You want me to pick you up?"

"That'd be good."

"All right. It's a date."

Luther raised his eyebrows and Alex laughed. "Relax. It's only a figure of speech."

Sam and Brenda gave Luther a ride home after school. Fortunately, Vic was nowhere in sight. Luther felt pretty sure that his stepfather would never lay a hand on him, but after the previous night, he felt safer keeping his distance.

Remembering Brenda's comment from yesterday, Luther put on his better jeans and a fresh T-shirt instead of his usual bird clothes. With luck, he thought, none of the raptors will crap on me today.

Alex swung by in her mom's old Subaru about four o'clock. Roadkill jumped into the backseat and Luther sat up front.

"I've really been looking forward to this," Alex said as they drove the mile to Kay's. "I've never seen raptors up close, except for the dead ones my dad brings home."

"Does he find a lot?"

"Well, he did in Billings. People would bring them to him or he'd run across them when he went out to check on the duck and deer hunters. I guess most people around here bring them to Kay's, huh?"

"Yeah. Everyone knows she's the 'raptor woman.'"

Alex parked in Kay's empty driveway.

"I thought Kay would be here," Luther said. "She must be out on a call."

"Should we do this another time?" Alex asked.

"No, I just wanted you to meet her."

Luther got out and opened the back door for Roadkill. The dog shot out of the car and raced off toward the eagle pens.

"He needs to check everything out," Luther explained. He led Alex to the back porch, where he found the plastic box waiting for him.

"What's in there?" Alex asked.

"Mice."

"Yum. Sounds delicious."

"They're not so bad. The birds really like them."

As they walked toward the owl house, Alex said, "This is some place. Was it like this when Kay moved in?"

"The sheds were here, but they were pretty beat up. She's done a lot of work to get everything in shape. I've helped a little."

"What's in here?" Alex asked.

Luther opened the door to the owl house and they stepped inside. "Meet Elroy and Gopher."

Alex blinked as her eyes adjusted to the dim light. Then, she saw the two owls. "They're so *beautiful,*" she whispered.

"You can talk normally," Luther told her. "They're used to people."

"What kind of owls are they?"

Luther opened the plastic box and pulled a mouse out by the tail. He was feeling better now that he was out at Kay's again. Alex's presence definitely helped, too. "Elroy's a great horned owl," Luther told her. "And Gopher's a burrowing owl."

"They are so cool!"

Luther felt a surge of pride as he opened the door to Elroy's compartment. "Hey, Elroy," he cooed, extending the mouse to him. The owl gulped it right down.

"Oh jeez." Alex scrunched up her face. "So much for eating dinner tonight."

"Hey, it's more appetizing than shoveling horse poop," Luther said. "You want to feed him one?"

Alex reached out and picked up one of the dead mice.

"Try not to act nervous. The birds pick up on that," Luther told her.

"Oh right. This thing's about to bite my fingers off and I shouldn't be nervous?"

Alex slowly moved the dangling mouse toward Elroy's beak. When it hung two inches away, Elroy's head darted forward and he snatched it.

Alex jerked her hand back. "Yikes!"

Luther laughed. "See? Nothin' to it."

Next, Luther took her to see the eagles, then the hawks. Alex asked a ton of questions about each bird. He knew most of the answers, but a couple of times he lost his train of thought. Alex's blue eyes and dimple distracted him. He tried to keep his focus, but when she looked at him with her intense gaze, his heart fluttered like a hovering red-tail. As they left Hawk Heaven, Luther said, "I've been saving the best for last."

"Is this the part of the tour where you feed yourself to the birds?" Alex asked with a twinkle in her eyes.

"Very funny."

Luther led Alex to the falcon house. When they stepped

inside, Alex reached out and touched his arm. "Wow..." she whispered.

They both looked at the birds for a moment. A warm spot spread up Luther's arm from Alex's hand.

"They're falcons, aren't they?"

"Yeah..." said Luther, trying to keep his concentration. "This one's a peregrine. The one over here's a kestrel, and that one's a prairie falcon."

Alex leaned in close to the wire mesh and studied each bird. "They're really different sizes, aren't they?"

"Yeah. Part of that's because they're different species, but some are males and others are females. Female raptors are almost always bigger than the males."

"Are the female brains also bigger?" Alex asked. "Or is that only in humans?"

"No, but their mouths are definitely bigger," Luther shot back with a grin.

Before Alex could respond, she spotted the gyrfalcon.

"That," Luther told her, "is Sal."

"Oh..." Alex stepped close to Sal's cage and the falcon shifted its wings nervously. "Is this the bird you and Kay have been flying?"

Luther nodded proudly. "Yeah."

"I had no idea how big gyrfalcons were," Alex said. "And look at those amazing colors. I'd give anything to see her fly."

The words leaped out of Luther's mouth before he had time to think them through. "Let's do it," he said.

Alex turned an enthusiastic face toward him and asked "Really?"

Luther hesitated. Even though Kay had never specifically said so, he knew he absolutely was not supposed to fly Sal without Kay present. On the other hand, he'd already flown Sal a half a dozen times more or less on his own. What was the big deal? If he had any further doubts, Alex's sapphire-colored eyes cinched it for him.

"Sure," he said.

Twelve

uther walked back to the main house and collected the hood, heavy glove, and flying lure. He also grabbed a few pieces of quail breast to reward Sal with. Even as he hurried back to the falcon house, bats flapped in his stomach. He debated changing his mind, but the idea of flying Sal on his own—and with Alex present—proved too strong to resist. "I'll just do a couple of quick turns around the field and then put her back," he told himself.

Alex was waiting next to Sal's cage when he returned. He put on the glove like he'd done a dozen times before and stepped into the cage. Sal shifted her feet and studied him and Alex.

"Good girl," Luther told the bird. "This is going to be fun."

"Has she ever bitten you?" Alex asked from outside the cage.

"No. Not yet, anyway," Luther said, placing his hand at the base of the bird's breast. She stepped up obligingly.

"That's the way," he told the gyr, grabbing her jesses between his thumb and forefinger. "You're doing great."

Feeling more confident, Luther took the hood and quickly slipped it over Sal's head. As he tightened it, Alex asked, "She just lets you do that?"

"She's used to it. Kay's worked with her a lot. Birds of prey are really smart, and they learn fast. You ready?"

"Sure," Alex exclaimed.

Roadkill trotting behind them, they walked out into the field. Luther's heart raced as they reached Kay's favorite flying spot. "Here's the big test," he said to himself. As he removed Sal's hood, he suddenly remembered he'd forgotten to attach the radio transmitters to Sal's jesses. He glanced back at the main house and considered going back for them, but Sal looked eager to fly. Her black eyes gleamed in the smoky sunlight and she twisted her head, alert to every movement and noise.

Luther knew he should go back to get the transmitters but decided the odds were heavily against her flying away. She's never shown any inclination to leave before, he assured himself.

"You might want to stay back a little," Luther said to Alex. She retreated a few steps and squatted next to Roadkill, putting her arm around the Border collie.

"Okay. Here goes."

He released Sal's jesses and with a quick upward thrust of his arm sent the gyr airborne. Sal's wings flashed in the sun as she shot across the field. She sped in a wide loop and for a sickening moment, looked like she might just keep on going. At the edge of the field, though, she banked sharply and flew to her favorite spot on the dead snag.

Alex gasped. "She's amazing."

Luther took a deep breath and then exhaled. "Yeah. But just wait."

Uncoiling the lure, he began swinging it around his head, shouting "Hup!"

"You're not going to try lassoing that poor bird are you?" Alex asked.

Luther let the end of the lure out to its full extension. "This is a training lure."

"For who? You or the bird?"

"It builds up her strength and coordination."

Luther continued to twirl the lure. Sal watched from the perch for a moment and then shot forward. She rocketed toward the lure and, at the last second, Luther jerked it away, yelling "Ho!" The lure fell to the ground, and Sal flew two laps of the field before returning to her perch.

Alex stepped closer. "No wonder you love coming out here so much. This is great!"

Luther tried to hide his pleasure. "Kay can keep the lure going when Sal misses," he said. "I'm still just learning how to do this."

"It looked good to me. Why do you yell 'Ho!'?"

"It's to let her know that there's still something to hunt."

"You mean, you're training her to kill cute little bunnies and tweetie birds?"

"Pheasants and ducks, too. Sal's so big and fast, she can race down almost any kind of small game."

"I'll bet the animal rights people love that."

"It's no different than any other hunting," Luther responded. "And in a way, it's more natural. But I don't really care about the hunting that much. I just like to see her fly."

"I see how you got hooked," Alex said, slipping her finger beneath her necklace.

Again, Luther whirled the lure over his head. Sal crouched on the perch and watched him. "Come on, girl," he called. "Come on."

Once more, Sal launched herself off the snag. But this time, only ten feet out from the tree, the gyr plummeted.

For a split second, Luther thought Sal must have seen some real food on the ground below or grown tired of the lure. Then, he saw her wings lose control and her body tumble end over end. Right before Sal hit the ground, he heard it.

A shotgun blast.

Luther's heart seized. He looked at Alex, whose mouth hung open, and then at Roadkill, who'd leaped to his feet. At first, Luther couldn't piece it together. The lure dropped from his hands and he looked back toward Sal.

Then, his legs were flying. He crossed the hundred yards as if he were floating, the sickness rising higher in him with every step. He prayed that what he knew he'd seen hadn't really happened.

But it had. As he skidded to a halt, he saw Sal on the ground, blood splattering her silver-streaked breast. Her smoky eyes stared at him, unseeing.

Alex ran up behind him, breathing hard. "Oh my god."

Luther knelt next to the falcon and reached out his hand. Sal's warm blood seemed to soak into his fingertips. The gyr's feathers were still warm. Luther half-expected her to get up and fly, but he knew.

She was dead.

Luther tried to get his brain to work, but it wouldn't turn over. When Alex touched his shoulder, he looked up at her. Her eyes were wet and tears dribbled down her cheeks. Luther's own eyes felt like dust.

He stood and looked down at the bird, then at the river. "Down there," he said, pointing toward the brush.

"Wait!" Alex said. "It might not be safe. Let me go call my dad."

"Use Kay's phone. I'll meet you back here," Luther said, his legs already moving.

Alex ran back toward Kay's house as Luther and Roadkill rushed toward the trail that led to the riverbank. The river was the only place the shooter would have had a clear view of the snag without being seen from the field. Luther slowed as he entered the willows, looking to both sides. Then, he stopped to listen. All he could hear was the river washing along the bank ahead of him.

He continued running to the river's edge. He scanned the bank in both directions and began walking downstream. About twenty yards down, in the mud of the riverbank, he found the footprints. They looked like they were from work boots—the same kind worn by half the people in Heartwood.

Luther followed the boot prints for a few yards, but they

disappeared onto hard ground baked dry by the drought. He kept searching along the bank. Willows grew so thickly he couldn't see more than five or ten feet ahead, but every few feet game trails entered the brush. Luther realized the shooter or shooters could have taken any one of them. After fifteen minutes, he hadn't discovered any more footprints or other clues so he gave up and turned back.

When Luther reached the field, Alex's father was squatting down, examining Sal's body.

"Luther," Alex said. "This is my dad."

Officer Matthews stood. "I'm sorry about your bird," he said.

"She's not mine," Luther said, his throat scraping out the words. "She's Kay's."

"Did you see anything?"

Luther shook his head. "No sir. She just started flying toward me and then dropped. A second later, I heard the blast."

Officer Matthews frowned. "Just what Alex said."

"But I did find footprints down by the river. They look fresh."

"Let's take a look."

Luther led Alex and her dad to the river. He showed them the boot tracks and where they disappeared onto hard ground. Then they searched the area for empty shell casings or anything else the shooter might have left behind. They found nothing and returned to where Sal lay dead.

"Do you think you can match the boot prints?" Luther asked.

Officer Matthews took off his cap and wiped the sweat from his forehead. "It might be possible, Luther, but to tell you the truth, the Fish and Wildlife Department isn't the FBI. Maybe the feds could figure out something, but those prints could belong to almost anyone around here."

Luther nodded. The reality of what happened began to spread through every part of him. Even worse, he knew it was one person's fault. His own.

"Do you have any idea who might have done this?" Alex's father asked, replacing his cap.

Luther remembered Warren Juddson's threats, but would Warren even stoop this low? Luther couldn't make himself believe it. It seemed more likely that someone else had done it—someone with a real grudge against Kay, or against environmentalists in general. Besides, Luther realized, Warren would still be at football practice.

"I don't know," Luther said. "Probably not."

Officer Matthews looked at Luther. "Well, think about it. I'll give you my number. Call me if anything comes to mind."

Alex's dad pulled a business card from his wallet and handed it to Luther.

Just then, they heard Godzilla grinding up the road. The green International turned into the drive, but instead of parking, Kay steered across the bumpy field and stopped near them. Luther's whole body began to tremble.

Roadkill ran over to Kay as she got out of the truck.

"Hey, boy," she said, scratching the dog's head. "Hi, everyone. What's all the excitement?"

Ten feet from them she stopped, her eyes riveted on Sal. She slowly stepped closer, and Luther, Alex, and her dad moved back. Kay swept a strand of her hair back behind one ear and then knelt next to her bird. She silently ran her hand over Sal's wing. After a long pause, she stood. Luther expected to see tears, but Kay's face was rigid.

"Tell me what happened."

"It's my fault," Luther said. Kay stared at him. "I wanted to show Alex what Sal could do. We brought her out here, and I was swinging the lure."

Luther again stopped and waited for someone to say something. No one did.

He swallowed and continued. "Everything went okay at first. Then, as she left the perch…"

Kay looked at Luther and then at Alex. "Did anyone see who did it?"

Alex's dad spoke. "Neither of them saw anything. Luther here found some tracks by the river. We may be able to use those."

Kay bent over and picked up the dead gyr. She cradled it in her hands, then looked up. "Alex, I'd like to talk to your dad for a few minutes, alone."

Alex nodded and stepped back.

"Do you want me to take care of Sal?" Luther asked.

"Luther," Kay said, without looking at him, "I think you're done here today."

"Okay. I'll come tomorrow after school."

"Don't bother," Kay said. "I'll take care of it."

Thirteen

L uther, Roadkill, and Alex walked toward Kay's house. Alex stopped at her mom's car, but Luther kept going.

"Wait, Luther," Alex said. "Let me give you a ride home."

"I'll walk."

"I'm so sorry." Tears again welled in Alex's eyes.

Luther paused and glanced back at Officer Matthews and Kay talking across the field.

"It wasn't your fault," Alex said. "You didn't kill Sal."

Yes I did. I killed her just like I pulled the trigger myself. To Alex, he simply said, "I'll see you tomorrow."

Leaving Alex behind to wait for her dad, Luther started down the road toward his house. Roadkill trotted ahead, plunging into the brush to investigate new scents, but Luther hardly noticed. The smoke blew thicker now, burning his eyes, and he almost welcomed the pain. "Is this real?" he kept asking himself. "Did that really just happen?" Unfortunately, the answer was always the same. This was something that wasn't ever going to "just get better."

"Why did I have to take Sal out?" he muttered, viciously kicking at a rock in his path. He tried to tell himself that the falcon needed the exercise, but that was a lie. He knew it was because he'd been showing off, and that because of it, Sal was dead.

Kay will never forgive me, Luther thought.

I'll never forgive myself.

Luther spoke to no one when he reached school the next morning, but when he walked into Current Topics, silence dropped over the classroom. He could tell word had gotten out about Sal. The way news traveled in Heartwood, probably everyone in town knew about it by now.

Luther didn't return his classmates' stares and didn't even glance at Alex. He just took his seat and pretended to read a book. He did notice that Warren's seat was empty.

After class, Alex caught up with him in the hall.

"Luther?" she asked. "How are you doing?"

He looked hard at her. "What do you care?"

Alex put her hand on his arm, but he pulled away.

"I care," she said. "I was there, remember? I know what happened."

"Yeah, you do," he said. "If I hadn't been trying to..."

Luther stopped himself and Alex's face changed.

"If you hadn't been trying to what?" she asked, her voice stiffening.

He paused, then waved his hand. "Nothing," he said. "Just leave me alone."

❧

Luther didn't even consider manning the SFS table at lunch. He was finished with that whole do-gooding fiasco. Instead, he took his lunch out to the baseball field and sat alone in the bleachers. The sun blazed orange overhead, and a sulfur-colored, smoky light saturated the field.

He kept rehashing the previous afternoon in his mind, but nothing made it any better. He thought about each decision and how things might have gone differently, but no matter what he told himself or how he attacked it, the bottom line came out the same. Sal was dead. Period. Forever.

And the more he thought about it, the more a chasm opened inside of him. Without the birds, this town held nothing for him. His home life—never great to begin with—had gone to hell after the blow-up with Vic. Since he quit football, his friends had drifted away one by one. School? Well, he got by, but he'd never been a star student except maybe in math, so what did that matter?

His mind again returned to the plan for getting out of Heartwood. Before, he'd always had something to lose. Now, he felt like he'd already left.

As he pondered where he might go, Luther suddenly felt someone's presence next to him. He squinted up into the sun and saw Chet.

"Hey," Chet said.

"Hey."

"Mind if I sit down?"

Luther waved his hand. "There's plenty of room."

Chet sat and stared out at the jaundiced field. "I heard about the falcon," he said. "I'm sorry."

Luther didn't reply.

"What happened," Chet said, "it sucks." His friend hesitated for a moment and then continued, "I also need to tell you something."

Luther thought Chet would bring up the SFS thing or their argument last week, but instead, Chet said, "I went down to Sky Burger yesterday about five o'clock. Warren was sitting at the next table with some of the guys."

Luther turned toward him, his throat tightening.

"Warren was talking low, but I could hear what he was saying. He was bragging about shooting something, and I'm pretty sure he was talking about your bird."

Luther didn't want to believe it. "He couldn't have. It happened during football practice."

Chet shook his head. "Warren was only there at the beginning and he didn't dress out. I heard him tell the coach he had a doctor's appointment."

Luther turned the information over in his mind. "You know where he is now?"

"No. But he'll be at football after school. The coach told him if he missed one more practice, he'd get benched."

A slow fury began building inside Luther as he returned his gaze to the field.

Chet stood. "Anyway, I thought you should know."
Luther nodded and Chet walked away.

Luther passed the rest of the day as if he were in his own space capsule. He walked to class, answered questions from teachers, and handed in his homework, but inside, his rage simmered. He'd never felt this way before—hot and icy at once—burning up, yet coldly calculating strategy and tactics. He played over different scenarios, preparing his mind and body for conflict, and he wondered if this was how soldiers felt before battle.

Before he knew it, the final school bell sounded. He left class quickly and went to his locker. He shoved his pack and sweatshirt into the tiny space and jammed the door shut. Then, taking care to avoid Alex, he walked out the front door of the school and waited to the side where he wouldn't be noticed. He knew that anyone coming into the school had to pass this way.

The rush of students going home began to slacken, and Luther watched intently. As he waited, the image of Sal falling out of the sky replayed again and again in his mind. Suddenly his eyes focused on a familiar shape strutting toward school. Dressed in his letterman's jacket, Warren Juddson crossed the street and then the parking lot, heading for the school's front doors. Luther's mind and body twisted tight and he moved to intercept him.

A few students still milled around the front entrance,

and Warren didn't spot Luther until he was about twenty yards away. Luther saw Warren's body tense, and if he had any doubts about who killed Sal, they vanished. Still, Warren tried to keep cool as Luther walked closer. When they were about five yards apart, Warren said. "Well, look who's here. The eco-fre—"

Luther swung as hard as he could and connected with Warren's jaw and cheek. A searing pain shot from the base of Luther's little finger. Caught off guard, Warren reeled back. With both hands, Luther grabbed the collar of Warren's shirt and drove his knee into his groin.

Luther's knee hit slightly off target, but it made Warren gasp and curl forward. As he did, he threw his arm around Luther's neck and dragged him to the sidewalk.

"You bastard!" Warren growled, blood pouring from his mouth. He tried to drive Luther's face into the cement, but his hold slipped and Luther twisted free. Warren dove after him and swung. If Warren had fully connected, Luther would've been out cold, but the punch only clipped his nose, causing blood to cascade down his shirt. As Warren recovered his balance, Luther threw another punch with his left. The blow grazed Warren's ear, and Warren sprang at Luther with a full body block, knocking the breath from him and driving him backward into a hedge.

Warren pulled back and readied a swing, but Luther managed to dodge to the side and the blow missed. He dropped to the ground and scrambled forward on all fours. Warren lunged at him, but Luther escaped. He leaped to his feet first and kicked Warren as hard as he could in the ribs. The kick stunned Warren, and before he could recover, Luther kicked him again in the same spot.

Warren rolled over, groaning. As Luther drew back for another kick, two pairs of arms grabbed him and yanked him back.

"You killed Sal!" Luther yelled at the top of his lungs. "You killed my bird!"

Warren started to his feet, but two football players and an assistant coach intercepted him. The two sets of arms continued to drag Luther back. "You son of a bitch!" Luther screamed. Then tears scalded his eyes.

Luther was sitting on his bed when he heard Vic drive up. Vic had been away the night before, fighting a flare-up in the Sapphires south of town. As he heard his stepfather enter the house, Luther braced himself for another assault, but instead he heard the muffled voices of Vic and his mother talking quietly. After a few minutes, the door to Luther's room opened, and his stepfather walked in.

Vic paused to study his stepson's purple nose and the cast that encased his hand, forearm, and smallest two fingers. Then, he walked over and sat at the end of Luther's bed.

"You all right?"

Luther shrugged and stared down at his damaged hand, still half-expecting a total ass-chewing. Besides breaking the fifth metacarpal in his little finger—a classic "boxer's fracture," the doctor had told him—he'd been given a one-week suspension from school.

"I heard about Kay's falcon," Vic said. "I'm sorry. If Warren did it, he stepped over the line."

"He did it."

His stepfather nodded. "I can't say I approve of how you reacted, but I understand why you did it and—"

Luther looked over at him.

Vic scratched his day-old beard, staring at his stepson as if he had something important or personal to say. But instead, he stood and said, "Anyway, Luther, your mom and I talked this thing through and decided you need to come up with a plan for how you're going to spend the next week. Even though we understand why it happened, we take this suspension very seriously and expect you to do something positive with the time, understand?"

"I got it."

"That cast doesn't look like it will keep you from getting some things done."

"No..."

"Good. I head back to the fire line in the morning, so you can start by cleaning up around the yard. I want you to cut back all the brush around the house so in case a fire comes this way, we won't have to worry about it."

Luther nodded and Vic left.

Fourteen

The next day, Friday, Luther rose at his usual time even though he'd been suspended. He dressed, shuffled into the kitchen, and turned on the radio. As he ate his cereal, he learned that firefighters were having some success with the Demming blaze.

His mom came in. "Any news about the fires?"

Luther swallowed. "They've built a good line around the western edge of the Demming fire. That should keep it away from Heartwood."

"Is the rest of it under control?"

"More than 80 percent contained. They also said the Rocky Gulch blaze has about burned itself out."

"Well, that is good news," his mother said.

A few minutes later, Luther heard a car pull up and then a knock on the door. He opened it to see Mrs. Saperstein, the school counselor. He was expecting her. After Luther's fight with Warren, the principal had arranged for her to come out and pay the Wrights a visit. The smoke wasn't as thick this morning, so the counselor, Luther, and his mom sat on the front porch.

After exchanging pleasantries with Luther's mom, Mrs. Saperstein said, "So Luther, tell me about the fight."

He started from the beginning. He told her about Warren's threat to shoot Kay's birds, his arguments with Warren at the SFS table, his wrecked bicycle, and what had happened to Sal. The counselor agreed that those were extenuating circumstances, and to Luther's surprise, she didn't bawl him out or anything. She wrote down some notes on a pad of paper and then slipped her pen back into her purse.

"I want to give your case some thought," she told Luther. "If Warren did shoot your falcon, that is very serious. On the other hand, your own response was in some ways no better than Warren's actions. Violence only breeds more violence. That may sound like a cliché, but it's true. What happened is awful, but you had a choice in how to respond."

"I agree," Mrs. Wright chimed in, looking sternly at her son.

Luther nodded.

"I will probably come up with some recommendations. Meanwhile," Mrs. Saperstein continued, "I hope you'll think hard about what happened and why you did what you did. Also, how you might have handled the situation more positively."

Luther promised that he would and the counselor left. A few minutes later, his mom hurried off to work. After her car pulled away, Luther changed into his work clothes and walked out to the garage. He was about to grab the wheelbarrow handles when he stopped, remembering what Alex had said about finding more evidence before accusing Vic or anybody else of arson.

Luther began poking around the garage to see if he could discover anything incriminating. He opened cabinets, examined boxes and utility shelves along the wall, and searched everywhere else he could think of. He found an arsenal of items that could be used for starting fires — gasoline, flares, motor oil, even some old blasting caps. All of it, however, was stuff that could be found in almost any garage in Heartwood.

The only thing that seemed the slightest bit suspicious was a can of kerosene that had been shoved back behind some boxes. Kerosene was used for a lot of things, but he'd never seen Vic use it. Also, Vic had specifically said "kerosene" when Luther had overheard him talking to Clifton Hanks a few days before. Still, it didn't prove anything and left Luther feeling more uncertain than ever.

"If only I hadn't overheard that conversation," he muttered to himself. With a sigh, he went back over to the wheelbarrow and awkwardly rolled it outside.

Before going to the fire line that morning, Vic had left Luther a list of what he wanted done around the place. Lawns formed a good fire buffer on the front and right sides of the house, but thick hedges bordered the garage and a large woodpile was stacked against the back wall of the house. All of it would have to be taken care of, and Luther decided to tackle the woodpile first.

His stepfather always cut their winter firewood himself, but often he went overboard. Two cords of wood sat next to the house and another couple of cords waited in a pile nearby, ready to be split. Luther decided to move the wood to a spot under a cottonwood tree, about a hundred feet from the house. It wasn't something he looked forward to. A hard and tedious task with two good hands, the job would be even more difficult with the cast. Despite all that, he threw himself into the work and spent the next two hours loading the wood into the wheelbarrow and pushing it over to the cottonwood tree, eight or ten pieces per load. The physical labor was exhausting, but provided relief from thinking about Sal and Kay. By the time Luther finished, his back ached and his injured hand throbbed.

"At least the smoke isn't too bad today," he told himself, taking a break to drink water from the hose. He let the cool water run over his head and face and then stood up to assess his progress. As soon as he did, though, he started thinking about Sal and the shooting all over again. He felt like walking over to Kay's to talk to her about it, but was afraid to, at least so soon. He wondered if Kay would ever speak to him after what happened. *I wouldn't blame her if she didn't. If I was Kay, I'd probably never want to see me again.*

To drive these thoughts from his head, Luther turned to the uncut woodpile. The rough logs were bigger and more difficult to handle since they hadn't been cut down to fireplace-size. Luther thought about trying to split them first, but their wood splitter was busted, and even though the cast left his thumb and first two fingers free, there was no way he could wield an axe. Instead, he just loaded the seventy-pound logs into the wheelbarrow and dumped them one by one next to the stacked wood under the cottonwood tree.

After finishing the woodpile, Luther dragged out Vic's smaller chainsaw, the one with the eighteen-inch blade, and filled it with gas and chain oil. He strapped on goggles and a safety helmet and then carried the saw to the side of the garage where the hedges crowded against the outside wall.

Luther flipped the ON switch, pulled out the choke, and tugged the starter cord. Vic kept all their tools in immaculate condition, and the saw fired up on Luther's second pull. Holding the saw steady was another matter.

Luther gripped the top bar with his left hand, but the cast on his right made it awkward to operate the trigger that served as the saw's "gas pedal." He tried several different handholds until he figured out one he could live with.

His mom had planted these hedges when they'd first bought the house, but both his parents had agreed that the fire danger outweighed their sentimental value. Luther crouched and began cutting the first bush at its base. After five seconds, the plant toppled undramatically.

"Timber!" Luther yelled, to amuse himself.

As he started in on the second hedge, Luther thought he heard a voice over the whine of the chainsaw but figured he must be imagining it.

Then, he distinctly heard someone shout his name.

Luther hit the kill switch and turned to see Chet standing fifteen feet behind him.

"Hi," Luther said, removing his helmet and his safety goggles.

"Hey," Chet said.

"Aren't you supposed to be in school?"

Chet pointed to his watch. "Lunch."

"Already?" Luther couldn't believe he'd worked past noon, but his rumbling stomach confirmed it. He set the saw down. "You want some juice?"

"Sure."

He led Chet into the house and poured a couple of glasses of OJ. They carried them out to the front steps and sat down.

"How's the hand?" Chet asked.

Chet's question seemed to make the throbbing in Luther's hand worse. "It's okay. I've got some painkillers if it gets too bad."

"Are you supposed to be working like that?"

"The doctor said it was all right as long as I didn't overdo it."

"Does that include cutting down trees?"

Luther chuckled. "Probably not."

Chet took another drink. "Everyone's talking about your fight with Warren. Did you hear he got suspended, too?"

That surprised Luther since Warren hadn't started the fight. "For fighting?" he asked.

"I'm not sure," Chet said. "But yeah, that, and I think the principal got wind of Warren killing your bird."

"Did someone turn Warren in?"

"I don't think so, but by now, everyone knows about it. The sheriff's been asking around town if anyone has any information."

Luther took a long swig of juice. Alex's father or Kay must have reported it, he thought.

"You seen Alex?" Luther asked.

"Yeah," Chet said. "A lot of people were asking her about what happened. She was setting up that table of yours when I came over here."

"She was?"

Chet nodded and drained his glass.

Luther suddenly felt ashamed of the way he'd acted toward her the day before.

"Luth, does Alex know about what happened between you and Warren?"

Luther knew Chet wasn't talking about Sal's shooting. He shook his head. "No, I haven't told her. I've been afraid to."

"I know I've said this before, but what happened, it could have been any of us."

Luther looked Chet in the eye. He knew his friend was trying to make him feel better, but inside, he didn't buy it. "I don't know that. Can you really say you would have gone along with Warren that night? That you would have done what he—what we—did?"

"Probably. Yeah. And it's not like it was the worst thing in the world. Things just got a little out of hand and you happened to be there at the time."

Luther took a deep breath and looked away. "Well,

whether that's true or not, it was wrong. And I'm the one who has to live with it."

"You're not the only one."

Luther snorted. "You mean Warren? That guy's got the conscience of a rock."

"Maybe," Chet said. "But why do you think he hates you so much now?"

Luther looked back at Chet. "He told me why. It's because he thinks I turned my back on the team."

"I don't think so. I think it's because every time he sees you, it reminds him that maybe he shouldn't have done what he did."

Luther's mouth opened, but no words escaped. He and Chet just sat silently for a moment looking at the hazy mountainsides to the north.

Finally, Chet set down his glass and stood up. "Anyway, I just wanted to stop by."

Luther also stood. "Thanks." He stuck out his right hand to shake, but then they both looked at the cast and laughed. "Yeah, well..."

Chet grinned. "Yeah. Catch you later."

Luther watched Chet go to his car and start it up. As Chet pulled out, he waved. Luther gave a little salute with his cast and carried the glasses into the house. After wolfing down a cheese sandwich, he went back outside to vanquish the hedges.

As he started up the chainsaw and began to cut, he didn't notice the wind picking up from the east.

Fifteen

fter obliterating the hedges and dragging their carcasses away from the house, Luther showered and
took one of the painkillers his doctor had prescribed. Ten minutes later, he lay down on his bed. Within
moments, he was out.

The drugs gave him especially weird dreams. Dreams
about flying and smoke and things he'd forgotten to do.
When the knocking started, Luther thought it was just part
of his hallucinations. Only when it grew louder did it start
to pull him out of the subterranean sleep world he'd been
exploring.

Suddenly he realized that someone was pounding on
the front door. He jumped out of bed and almost collapsed
as the blood rushed from his head.

"Whoa!" he muttered, clutching the doorframe. After
he regained his balance, he staggered to the front door and
opened it.

"Luther, what are you *doing?*" Alex's face was flushed
with worry and strands of her red hair hung limply over
her forehead.

"What do you mean?" he asked, confused.

"I tried calling, but no one answered. Don't you know about the fire?"

"The Demming fire?" he asked, trying to rev his brain up to speed. "They had it under control this morning." Looking beyond Alex, though, he saw thick clouds of smoke barreling westward.

"The winds kicked up, and it's jumped two fire lines. It's coming this way!"

"Kay and her birds! Are they okay?"

"I don't know, but I've got to get to the stables to see if someone let the horses out."

"Where are your parents?"

"They're both at work, and I couldn't reach anyone on the phone. Come help me with the horses, then I'll take you to Kay's."

Luther hesitated, thinking he should go directly to see about the birds. But he didn't have a car, and Alex's plan made more sense. The stables were closer to the fire. If they went there first, they should still have enough time to check on the raptors.

"Okay," he told Alex. "Let me get my boots on. Go to the garage and get my father's thirty-six-inch chainsaw, the big one with the green handle. There should also be a gas can and a bottle of chain oil there."

"Hurry!" Alex said.

Luther closed the front door, ran to his room, and quickly pulled on his boots.

"Dammit!" he shouted, fumbling with the laces. Having two fingers out of commission made him botch the knot and he had to start again. As he pulled on his heavy work jacket, Brenda burst through the door.

"Luther!" she said. "Do you know about the fire?"

"Yeah," he said, brushing past her. "Stay here! I'm going to the stables with Alex. Then we're going to Kay's."

"Luther, don't you dare leave! What if the fire comes here?"

"I cleared everything from around the house," he told her. "Just get out there with the hose and pour as much water as you can on the roof. And tie a wet rag around your mouth."

"Luther!" his sister protested.

"I'll be back as fast as I can. Try to call Mom at work and tell her to get home. Just don't panic and you'll be okay," he said and rushed out the door.

Despite the painkiller, adrenaline now flushed Luther's mind clear. He rushed to Alex's truck with Roadkill right beside him. He didn't want the dog along but figured the Border collie would be as safe with him as anywhere else. As he opened the passenger door, he glanced into the truck bed and saw the chainsaw and extra gas and oil sitting next to the wheel well.

"Come on!" Alex shouted as he and Roadkill jumped into the cab of the truck. The motor was already running, and Alex hit the gas even before Luther closed the door.

"How far's the fire?" he asked as they sped toward the main road.

"I don't know. A couple of miles, maybe less."

"Oh, man," he muttered. "Not good."

Alex steered the truck into a thick bank of smoke, and visibility plunged to a few yards.

"The turn's coming up," Luther warned her. Alex braked and, sure enough, the stop sign at the old highway appeared eerily in front of them. Ash rained down like snow over the windshield and hood of the car. Alex strained to see if any cars were coming from the left, but it was impossible to tell.

"How's it look on your side?" she asked.

"I don't know."

"Okay. Hang on!"

Alex gunned the engine and swung right, onto the pavement. Luther gritted his teeth, but no other vehicles were coming; Alex punched the accelerator toward the stables. Moments later, Luther thought he heard sirens and the sound of helicopters overhead. Straining his eyes upward, he saw only smoke and the ghosts of tree branches hanging above the road.

Suddenly the smoke lifted to reveal the stables before them.

Luther and Alex gasped.

A wall of flames engulfed the hillside behind the huge barn and in one spot almost reached the barn itself. The trees along the east side of the parking area hadn't yet caught fire, but it looked like they could go at any moment.

Alex jerked the truck left into the driveway and, gravel flying, skidded to a halt in the center of the parking area, as far from any structures as possible. Luther saw only one other car parked nearby.

"Do you see any horses?" Alex shouted, flinging open the driver's side door.

Luther and Roadkill had already leaped to the ground. "There's five out in that pen!" he hollered back, the crackling of the flames filling his ears. "How many horses are here?" he asked.

"Fourteen altogether!"

"What should we do?"

"Let's try to move them all into the same pen. I'll start getting them and when I bring them out, open that gate over there. But don't let the other horses escape. They'll probably try."

As Alex dashed into the barn, another woman jogged out leading a palomino. "Thank god someone else came!" she shouted. Luther and Roadkill rushed to the large pen and unlatched the gate. As it swung open, the woman let go of her horse and slapped it on the butt. The palomino trotted toward the five horses already in the enclosure.

"Can you help?" she asked Luther. He recognized her as the woman he'd seen jumping the spotted gray horse the first day he'd come to the stables.

"Yeah—until you get all the horses out."

"Thanks!" the woman shouted, already halfway back to the barn.

As Luther watched, the flames reached the back of the barn and a yellow snake of fire crawled toward the roof. With a startling roar, the trees across the parking lot burst into flame. Their needles sizzled and crackled as fire raced up through their branches toward their crowns. Even from this far away, he could feel a wall of heat slam his body.

"Come on, Alex," he muttered, pacing back and forth in front of the gate.

Just then, Alex emerged leading two horses by their halters, a gray Appaloosa and what looked like a quarter horse. Luther noticed Alex had thrown feed sacks over their eyes and figured it was to keep them calm.

He opened the gate again and Alex led the horses through. As soon as they were clear, she removed the feed sacks and let them go. They galloped toward the rest of the herd, which had gathered at the far end of the pen.

"How many's that?" Alex shouted.

"Eight! Do you want me to come help you?"

"No! I need you to open and close the gate."

"The barn's already burning!"

"I know!" Alex sprinted toward it just as the woman led another horse out.

"Why doesn't she get two at a time?" Luther grumbled. At this rate, they were never going to get all the horses out. As Luther again opened the gate, Roadkill nipped at the legs of the horse, driving it through.

By now, flames covered more than half of the back wall of the barn, and the trees across the parking lot blazed like sixty-foot torches. Black smoke blotted the sun. Luther thought of Mordor, that dark evil land from *The Lord of the Rings*.

When Alex emerged with her own horses, Sugar and

Diamond, Luther felt a wave of relief. As awful as it would be to lose any horses, it would be almost unthinkable to lose Alex's.

"Hurry!" he shouted to her.

Besides covering their eyes, Alex had clipped a snap-on lead to Diamond's halter. She had to tug on the horse to get him to cooperate, but with Roadkill's help, she finally managed to get both horses through the gate. As soon as she unclipped Diamond's lead, the two horses rushed off to join the others. Just then, a huge ball of flame burst out of the edges of the metal roof. The roar of the inferno blasted Luther's ears, and the barn began to creak and groan.

Luther closed the gate and hollered, "Come on!"

He and Alex ran toward the barn entrance. The woman appeared at the doorway in tears. "I tried to get the big bay," she sobbed, "but it wouldn't come!"

"Let's try to drive them out!" Alex yelled at Luther.

Luther hesitated for an instant, then shouted, "Roadkill, stay!" The Border collie barked and raced back and forth but was frightened enough to obey.

When Luther followed Alex into the barn, he couldn't believe what he saw. Orange, yellow, and blue flames jetted across the top of the high roof, devouring the wooden beams. Two entire walls were aflame and, fed by stacks of dry hay, the stalls at the very end of the barn had turned into tinderboxes.

"Where are the last horses?" Luther shouted, running.

Alex stopped at a stall. "Right here! Try to get something over their eyes!"

The roof groaned overhead, and at the far end of the building a burning rafter crashed to the ground.

Luther threw open one of the stall doors. A terrified white bay reared and screamed in front of him.

"Come on! Go!" Luther shouted at the horse.

The horse didn't budge.

"Oh, man." Luther grabbed some loose reins that were hanging outside of the stall and slipped inside. The bay slashed at him with its front hooves. Dodging the deadly blows, he eased his way over to the side and whipped the reins at the horse's backside.

"Go! Get out of here!"

The horse reared again, then suddenly bolted out of the stall. Fortunately, it ran in the right direction and disappeared through the barn door to the outside.

As Luther stepped out of the stall, a second horse rushed by him and he staggered back to avoid being run over.

"Only one more!" Alex threw open the stall door to free the last horse. Two stalls away, a fresh flash of fire exploded. Luther glanced around. Everything seemed ablaze and the intense heat seared his skin. He felt like a casserole in a gas oven.

"Help me!" Alex shouted.

Inside the stall, a brown and white paint cowered against the back of the stall. Luther was surprised the horse wasn't trying to kick down the walls.

"Slap him on his butt with the reins!" Alex shouted.

Keeping a close eye on its rear hooves, Luther lashed at the horse. Meanwhile, Alex got in front of the horse, threw her jacket over his eyes, and pulled on his halter.

"Why isn't he moving?" Luther yelled. Another timber crashed to the ground, no more than thirty feet from them.

"The stall's his safe place! He doesn't want to budge!"

"That's crazy!"

"Slap him harder!"

Luther whipped the horse's flank with all his might, and suddenly, the horse bolted, throwing Alex and her jacket to the ground.

Luther rushed to help Alex up. "Are you okay?"

"I'm fine! Let's get out of here!"

Together they raced toward the entrance. Flames seemed to explode on every side of them and smoke from the oily hay filled Luther's lungs. Just about when he expected his skin to ignite, he and Alex burst through the open barn door.

It took Luther a moment to get his bearings. Flames raged all around him. Black smoke had turned the sky dark as night.

The woman was already in her car and as soon as she saw Luther and Alex safely emerge from the barn, she waved and gunned the engine out of the parking area. Luther looked out at the pen and could make out most of the horses huddled at the far end. A few pieces of knap-weed smoldered inside the pen, but the animals looked like they'd be safe.

"Come on," he said. "Let's get to Kay's."

"Do you see the three horses we turned out?" Alex asked.

Luther looked all around him, but saw no sign of them. "No!"

"Okay. Let's get out of—*Luther watch out!*"

Luther spun around just in time to see the brown and white paint charging toward him. He leaped to the side, but the horse wasn't aiming for him. He was running back toward the barn.

"YEE-HAAA!" Alex screamed, trying to turn the horse.

It didn't work. The horse galloped through the doors into the flaming barn.

Alex started after it, but Luther grabbed her. "No!" Just then, the ground shuddered and a hideous, high-pitched moan filled the air.

Luther pulled Alex back. "Run!" he yelled.

They sprinted away from the barn, Roadkill barking and running with them. Luther glanced over his shoulder as the barn's enormous roof crashed toward earth. In what seemed like slow motion, the roof crushed the rest of the barn, caving in walls and launching burning logs and boards in all directions. Luther and Alex reached the end of the drive and turned just as the roof thundered to the ground.

"Oh my god!" Alex gasped. "That horse!"

Just then, a huge beam flew out of the flames. Like a missile, it slammed into Alex's pickup truck, piercing the gas tank. Fuel exploded, engulfing the truck in an orange and blue fireball.

Roadkill barked furiously.

"Not the truck too!" Alex said, stunned. "God, if we'd been—"

"Come on!" Luther said. "We've got to get to Kay's!" But as he said it, he knew it was hopeless. On foot, they'd never reach her place in time. The fire had already burned beyond the stables and at this rate would be at Kay's in twenty, thirty minutes at most.

Alex seemed to snap out of her shock. "We'll take Diamond!" she shouted at Luther.

"What? We don't even have a saddle!"

"We don't need one!"

"Shouldn't we take Sugar instead?"

"Diamond's our only chance! Sugar's too slow and she's not strong enough to carry both of us. With your cast, you'll have to ride with me!"

Before Luther could object, Alex hopped the gate and ran toward the herd of horses at the far end of the pen. As Luther watched, she flung the snap-on lead over the top of Diamond's neck and clipped it to both sides of the halter. Using the lead as reins, she scrambled onto Diamond's back. The horse twirled, but she got him under control. Luther swung open the gate and Alex trotted out.

As Diamond shuffled and pranced, Luther re-latched the gate. Alex leaned down and held her left hand toward him.

"Hook your left arm in mine and jump up!" she shouted.

Luther thought of jumping off the Heartwood bridge into the river. "If you think about it too much, you'll never do it," he told himself. He took four running steps, grabbed Alex's arm and leaped. He jumped too hard and almost slid right over Diamond's back, but Alex managed to keep him from falling off.

"Hold on to me!" she shouted. Luther needed no encouragement. Alex spurred the horse and they bolted forward.

"Come on, Roadkill!" Luther yelled.

Luther had never ridden bareback, and he felt like he was sitting on a mass of greased worms. Alex headed Diamond out the drive and onto the old highway, and with every stride of the horse, Luther expected to fly face first into the ground. Once on the road, though, the horse steadied into a canter, his hooves clattering against the pavement. Luther gripped the horse with his legs and began to adjust his body to Diamond's rhythm.

"You all right?" Alex shouted back.

Luther clutched her shirt and pressed his face against her neck. Even with the smoke, he could faintly smell her berry-scented shampoo. A thrill ran through him.

"I'm fine!" he shouted. "Where's Roadkill?"

"He's running right next to us!"

A Forest Service fire truck with its red lights flashing passed slowly going the opposite direction. Diamond shied away from it, but Alex kept him moving forward. To their right, the fire was racing along the mountains toward town. To the left, along the river, it burned more slowly. After a couple of minutes, they passed the forward edge of the flames.

When they reached the shortcut to Kay's house, Luther shouted, "Turn here!"

Alex turned Diamond to the left and they galloped along the path. A minute later, they emerged onto Elk Flats Road.

Sixteen

Smoke and ash choked Luther as they galloped through the swirling wind. One moment, he could see a hundred yards ahead of him, the next moment only ten. Without Roadkill, they might have missed the drive, but the Border collie led them straight to the house. Godzilla was nowhere in sight.

"We're cutting it close," Luther shouted, sliding off the horse. "You'd better get Diamond out of here! This is all going to burn, but if you take him down to my house and leave him with Brenda, he ought to be safe."

"What about you?" Alex objected.

"I'll be okay!"

Alex looked down at him, doubtful.

"Go!"

Reluctantly, Alex turned Diamond and spurred him forward. "I'll bring someone back to help!"

Luther watched her vanish into the smoke and then asked himself, "Now what do I do?"

Saving the birds was top priority. Luther ran around to the back porch to see if Kay had any boxes. He found an old dog kennel on the porch, but nothing in the house.

"Crap," he muttered, quickly counting up the number of birds he had to take care of. "This won't be enough."

Kay's pigeons could fend for themselves since they were free to come and go as they wanted. A couple of the raptors were also about ready to strike out on their own, but he still needed eight boxes to get the remaining birds. Even if he shoved two or three of them in the kennel, he'd be far short. Also, where was he going to put them? If the fire came through here, nothing would be safe.

From the back porch, Luther scanned Kay's property, looking for a place to put the birds. Sage, knapweed, and other brush grew almost everywhere. Then, he saw one place with bare ground—the eagles' large pens. The birds might just stand a chance in there, he thought. He picked up the heavy leather bird glove and the kennel and raced out to the owl house. Roadkill ran along next to him, frantically nipping at his heels.

"No game!" Luther shouted, but Roadkill kept nipping and Luther realized it wasn't playfulness, but fear that possessed the dog.

Inside the owl house, Luther slipped the glove over his left hand, then opened the door to Elroy's cage. He stepped in, and the great horned owl greeted him by bobbing his head up and down.

"Okay, Elroy, it's make or break time. I hope you're ready." He placed the glove at the base of Elroy's chest and after a moment the owl stepped up. Luther carried the owl outside, pointed him west, and swung his hand gently upward. He'd never done this with an owl before and didn't know if it would work, but Elroy needed little encouragement. He leaped off Luther's hand and flew into the smoke, away from the direction of the fire.

"One down," Luther said.

He stepped back inside the owl house and tried to coax the burrowing owl onto his hand, but Gopher wouldn't cooperate. After a few attempts, Luther seized the bird with both hands. Gopher bit Luther's cast, but he stuck the owl safely into the kennel and ran with it to Max's cage. Max paced nervously at the far end of the enclosure.

"It's okay, Maxie," Luther said to the golden eagle. "I'm just bringing you some company." Glancing around inside the pen, he spotted a rabbit hole near the opposite fence line. Luther slid Gopher out of the kennel and shoved him into the hole.

"Stay!" he ordered, knowing the bird had no idea what he was talking about, but to Luther's amazement, the owl blinked and scooted down out of sight in the burrow.

Luther next ran to Hawk Heaven. The goshawk and Alice the Cooper's hawk were almost fully recovered from their injuries, so he carried them out and tossed them up into the air. Like Elroy, Alice immediately took off into the smoke. The goshawk, however, flew to a corner post of Max's pen and perched there, staring uncertainly at the surreal surroundings.

Luther returned inside and placed the pair of red-tails in

the kennel. He carried the two birds to Max's pen and, since neither could fly, just dumped them on the ground as far as possible from the eagle.

"Don't hurt them," he told Max, realizing that the red-tails would make a nice snack for a normal golden. He hoped, however, that the poisoning had reduced Max's aggressive instincts enough that the eagle would leave the other birds alone.

Luther next carried the kennel to the falcon house. Since none of the three falcons could fly either, he threw open the cages one by one and stuffed the birds into the kennel together. As he picked up the peregrine, it sunk its talons into Luther's left hand.

"Ach!" Luther screamed, almost throwing the bird into the kennel. Blood dripped down his fingertips, but he didn't have time to worry about it. He raced back to Max's pen and released the last three birds onto the ground. Stepping back out and closing the wire door behind him, he saw four deer—a buck and three does—running west across the field.

The flames are almost here, he thought, stuffing the heavy bird glove into the waist of his jeans.

Kay had two outside faucets with hoses on the property, one attached to the main house, the other near Max's pen. Luther opened the second one full blast and dragged the hose over to the pen. He soaked the wooden posts—noticing that the goshawk had finally taken off—and sprayed the ground inside the pen. A couple of the birds shrieked their annoyance and moved away, but none of them were trying to eat each other.

That's something at least.

Next he drenched Max's shelter, fixing the hose so that water poured over the top of the eagle's shelter and onto the ground in front of the pen.

As soon as he got the hose in place, Roadkill began barking toward the east. Luther followed his stare, but the smoke blanketed the field like fog.

Then he saw it—an orange flash. At first, he couldn't tell what it was, but then he realized it was a large cottonwood bursting into flames near the river. Stunned, Luther watched the flames rocket from the bottom of the tree to its fifty-foot-high crown. An instant later, the tree next to it exploded into a fireball, followed by two trees on either side. Crackling sounds, like thousands of firecrackers, filled the air. Roadkill trembled against his legs.

Luther had hoped to be able to get some of Kay's belongings out of the house before the fire reached it—especially the drawings and manuscript for her raptor book—but time had almost run out. With fire about to consume everything, he realized that his best chance to save Kay's things was to save her house, and to do that, he had to take down the ponderosa pine before it caught fire.

As flames began igniting the sagebrush in the field, Luther rushed to Kay's back porch and grabbed her old chainsaw.

God, why didn't I finish servicing it when I had a chance?

Amazingly, Kay's saw still had gas in it. After flipping the switch to ON and pulling out the choke, Luther set the rusting heap on the ground. He awkwardly gripped the saw with his cast and used his good hand to pull the starter cord.

Nothing.

"Come on!" Luther yelled. He pulled the cord a second time, but the saw gave no sign of life.

Luther pushed the choke back in and yanked the cord. The motor sputtered and coughed this time, but then fell silent. When Luther pulled the cord a fourth time, the saw didn't even belch.

Devastated, Luther stood back up. "Now what?"

Even though he couldn't see the flames from the back porch, he knew they were almost on him. If he didn't get that ponderosa down, the house was a goner. "But if I can drop it," Luther told himself, "the house might have a chance."

He leaned over and tried the starter cord one more time. The saw burst to life.

"Yes!" Luther shouted, revving the engine with the gas trigger. He grabbed the saw's top bar with his good left hand, and despite a searing jolt in his right hand, used it to grasp the back handle. Doing his best to ignore the pain, he carried the idling saw to the base of the pine. Normally, he could drop a tree like this one in a couple of minutes, but with his damaged hand, he didn't know how he was going to manage. He decided to start with the easiest part—a straight-across cut that would reach about halfway into the trunk.

On the side of the tree away from the house, Luther jammed the chain into the bark and used his knee to prop the saw in place. Then, he used his right forefinger to pull the gas trigger. Fresh pain bolted up his right arm, but the chain whirred, spitting out sawdust as it dug into the tree. He finished the cut in less than a minute.

Thank god I at least sharpened the chain.

When the saw returned to idle, he heard Roadkill's shrill bark. Luther looked up and panic seized him. Fire had completely engulfed the field in front of him. Hawk Heaven—along with the falcon and pigeon houses—had turned into crackling bonfires. Flames licked the base of the owl house and, worse, covered the ground only thirty feet from where he stood.

Luther left the saw idling next to the tree and ran to the hose coming off the main house. He turned it on full bore, drenched his clothes and hair, and began spraying the house's walls. Within seconds, the weeds next to Kay's front door combusted. Luther attacked them one clump at a time, spraying them with water and kicking dirt at the flames. Twice his pants caught fire, but he doused the flames with the hose as soon as they erupted.

Roadkill raced back and forth, barking in a frenzy.

Luther at first didn't even notice the roof. Then, he glanced up and saw smoke curling from the wooden shingles. He aimed the hose at them, dousing the hottest spots, but the pine tree also looked ready to explode. He was just about to give up and abandon the place when he saw his mom's car rumble down the drive. Alex leaped out of the driver's door and ran to him.

"You're okay!" she yelled. "Your mom came home and

told me to take her car. She wanted to come, but she has her hands full at your place."

"I'm glad you're here!" Luther said, spraying water on Alex's hair and clothes. "Check on the birds!" he shouted. "They're in Max's pen!"

Dodging burning sage bushes, Alex ran toward the pen. Luther turned the hose on the pine tree, but he knew it was futile.

In a moment, Alex ran back. "They're okay. What can I do?"

A shingle caught fire on the roof.

"I've got to get up there!" Luther shouted, squirting the hose at the burning shingle. "Can you use a chainsaw?"

"No!" Alex said. "I think we should get out of here!"

"We can't. Everything Kay owns is in this house. We can save it. Just let me show you what to do."

Alex looked around fearfully at the flames.

"Over here," Luther said, leading her to the pine tree. "I made the first cut, but with this cast on my hand, I can't do the others." He pointed to the trunk. "You need to cut here, at an angle up from underneath so a wedge comes out. That's the direction the tree will fall. Then go to the other side, slice straight through to the wedge, and get out of the way."

"I guess I can try!"

"Be careful! Don't let the blade line up with your head. If it hits a knot and kicks up, it'll slice your face in two."

"Oh, jeez..."

"You can do it. I know you can." With his left hand,

Luther handed the still-idling saw to Alex and quickly showed her how to hold it. Leaving her to it, he sprinted to the back porch, dragging the hose behind him. He grabbed the small ladder Kay kept in back, threw it against the roof, and scrambled up with the hose. By the time he got on top, the roof had caught fire in four places. He crawled to the closest spot and tried to rip out a burning shingle by hand, but the flames and sparks burned his skin. Then he realized he still had the thick bird glove tucked into his waist. He yanked it out and slipped it back over his left hand. With the glove on, he ripped out the other burning shingles and threw them to the ground.

By the time he began squirting water on the roof's other hot spots, fire surrounded the house and, in fact, had raced more than a hundred yards past it. Luther coughed as he ripped out tiles. The smoke stung his eyes so badly he could barely keep them open. Burning sparks fell from the sky onto his neck, but he kept working. All the while the buzz of the chainsaw roared below him. When he got to the edge of the house next to the pine tree, he looked down.

Alex had sliced the wedge out of the tree and was starting in on the back cut. At first the saw chewed steadily, and with only a couple of inches to go, the ponderosa began to sway. Yes! Luther thought.

But suddenly the chain of the saw pinched and stopped. Alex gunned the motor and tried to wiggle it free, but the tree's weight pinned it tight. The engine stalled.

"Crap!" Luther said. The tree still swayed, but needed

a last shove to go down. "Leave it!" he shouted at Alex. "It might snap!"

His words had barely left him when a huge gust of hot air slammed into him. It drove a blizzard of sparks into Luther's face and, worse, into the branches of the tree. Needles caught fire in a dozen places and spread in a crackling fury. But the wind also sent the pine teetering away from the house.

"Get down from there!" Alex screamed.

Without thinking, Luther took a running start off the roof and threw himself at the tree. Ten feet off the ground, he collided with the trunk and held on. For a moment, the tree froze in place, flames licking Luther's face and body. Then, slowly, the pine began to lurch. He felt a sharp crack beneath him and the entire tree plummeted. Luther rode the trunk until the last moment and then tried to leap away.

His body hit something hard and the world went black.

Seventeen

uther tried to sit up, but pain shot through his left side and he fell back with a gasp. After recovering his breath, he lifted his right arm and saw that the cast was still there. Exploring with his free fingers, he also felt a plastic tube wrapped around his head with a tiny nozzle stuck into each of his nostrils. Bandages swaddled his left hand, both arms, and neck.

He tried to keep his breathing shallow, afraid of another jolt of pain, but he longingly eyed the glass of water sitting on a table beside his bed. His throat was so dry he could hardly swallow.

Just as he was trying to get up the courage to reach for the glass, his mom's smiling face appeared in the doorway. "You're awake!"

"I guess so," he muttered sleepily. "What day is it?"

"Saturday morning. You've been asleep since last night." His mother came over and put her hand on his forehead. "How do you feel? We've been so worried."

"Okay except for my side. What happened? What's this tube?"

"You broke three ribs, honey. The doctor says it's going to hurt for a while. The tube is for oxygen. That's to help with the smoke inhalation."

"Great." Luther lifted his left arm off the bed. "What are these?"

"You have a few second-degree burns and some kind of bite or cut on your hand. You also singed some eyebrows, but they say you'll be well enough to come home soon."

Luther reached up to his eyebrows and confirmed that, sure enough, they'd been roasted down to stubs. He asked his mother to hand him the glass of water, and he took a long, slow sip, welcoming the cool liquid on his parched throat.

"Is our house okay?" he asked.

"It's fine. But if you hadn't cleared away the woodpile and those shrubs, it probably would have burned. Vic came by earlier to see how you were, but he had to go back to help put out the hotspots."

"What about Kay's?"

"Alex has been waiting to see you. Why don't I let her tell you about it?"

When his mother left the room, Luther tried to reconstruct in his mind what had happened after he jumped into the burning tree. He vaguely remembered being trundled onto a stretcher at the hospital but not much else.

The door swung open and Alex walked in. "There he is," she said. "The Masked Marvel of Heartwood. You look very hip with those bandages on and the tubes stuck up your nose. How do you feel?"

"Like I've been hit by a tree."

"Well, that's pretty much what happened. Only it was you that hit the tree. Kay was just driving up as you leaped off the roof. I think her exact quote was that it was 'the wildest, stupidest, most crazy-assed thing' she'd ever seen."

Luther managed a lopsided grin.

"She's also really grateful," Alex added. "She said if you hadn't knocked that tree over, she would've lost everything."

"What happened?" he asked.

"You mean after you went free-diving off the roof?"

"Yeah."

"Well, let's see…" Alex plopped down in a chair next to the hospital bed. "If I remember correctly, you and the tree fell to the ground in a blaze of glory. Flames were shooting out everywhere. You rolled away from the trunk, but your clothes and hair were burning, so Kay and I— with a little help from Roadkill—dragged you away from the tree and doused you with the hose."

"My clothes were on fire?"

"For a few seconds you looked like a Roman candle."

"Very funny," he said. "What about the house? You saved the house?"

"Yep. And the birds are fine, too. A couple of the posts burned, but the fence around the eagle pen held. Kay went back to her place after your mom and sister got to the hospital. She said that when she got there the birds were all huddled around the small lake of water from the hose."

A load lifted off of Luther. "That's great."

"Even better, they cancelled school until Wednesday."

"Better for you maybe," Luther complained. "With my suspension, I don't get to be out there enjoying it."

"Well, that'll teach you to go attacking people—especially people with iron jaws."

Luther was quiet for a long moment. Then he said, "Alex, I need to tell you something."

Alex crossed her legs and leaned back. "You're not going to tell me that you really are a superhero, are you?"

"It's about Warren and Sal," he said. "It's about everything, really."

"What is it?" Alex said, her voice growing earnest as she straightened up in the chair.

Luther paused to collect his thoughts. "You know how you asked me why I quit the football team?"

"I remember."

"And I talked about that last game we played? Well, there was more to it than what I told you."

"I figured there was. But you don't have to tell me if you don't want to."

Luther tried to sit up, but sharp pains shot up from his rib cage. "No, I want to. It's something that's, uh, been on my mind for a long time. Too long."

"Okay."

"I've never told anyone else the whole story. Not even Chet." After another pause, Luther went on. "I think I told you that we lost the final game. We weren't supposed to.

The other team, they just had a great night and we made one bad mistake after another."

Alex nodded.

"Well, after the game, we were supposed to have a big celebration party out at this senior's house—Troy Mendehlson. He plays for Montana State University now, in Bozeman. Anyway, it was supposed to be this big good time to celebrate a victorious season and going on to regionals and everything."

"Except you lost the game."

"Right. We lost. The coach was furious. In the locker room, he said we'd thrown away a sure championship title. So when we all went to the party, instead of everyone being happy, this kind of ugly mood took over. The whole team just seemed on edge."

"Was everyone drinking?"

Luther absently rubbed the stubble of his eyebrows with his thumb. "Oh yeah. Big time. Troy's parents were out of town or something. After an hour or so it seemed like most people were drunk or stoned, trying to forget about the game. People were dancing on tables. Someone shoved an aluminum can down the garbage disposal. Troy had disappeared somewhere with his girlfriend so he didn't even know what was going on. Then, we ran out of alcohol."

"And that would be a good thing, wouldn't it?"

Luther grunted. "You'd think. It would've made sense to break up the party right then, but Warren and this senior named Chris Martin were just getting warmed up."

Alex's blue eyes stared back at him.

"Warren told Chris he knew where to get some booze. I was standing nearby so he asked me—well, told me—to come with them. I didn't really want to, but…hell, I don't know why I went."

"Were you drunk, too?"

"Not as bad as Warren and Chris, but yeah, I'd had a few. If I'd been sober, well, maybe I would have done something different. Anyway, I thought we were going to his house or a store or something—that maybe one of them had a fake ID. But instead, we drove out along the river. You know where all those new cabins have been built?"

Alex nodded.

"Well, Warren told Chris to turn in at one of the cabins. It was deserted. Most of them are just summer places and get closed up the rest of the year. I asked Warren what we were doing there, but he just said, 'Come on.' Chris took a tire iron out from under the seat of his truck and I followed them to the side door. Before I knew it, Warren had shoved the tire iron in along the door frame and splintered it open."

Alex's eyes widened. "What did you do?"

"I was so surprised I didn't do anything. My brain wasn't exactly functioning at top form. We went inside and Warren and Chris started rifling through all the cabinets looking for beer, wine—anything. Finally, I said something like 'Warren, I'm not sure this is a good idea,' but he just kept swinging open cabinets, hollering, 'These rich Californians got no right to be here anyway. They've got this coming to them.'"

Alex looked confused. "What rich Californians? Did he know who owned the cabin?"

"No. But you know how it is. People around here assume that anyone building a vacation home is from California. Anyway, we kept looking through the house and didn't find any alcohol. That *really* set Warren off. He and Chris started picking up lamps and vases and hurling them across the room. He kicked in a television set and even launched a table through the back window."

Alex raised her hand to her mouth.

"I know. It was bad, but the worst part of it was, I went along with it. I guess I rationalized to myself: 'Yeah, these people do deserve this. What right do they have coming here?' I think I even broke a clock or something."

Neither he nor Alex spoke for a moment.

"The thing I remember most clearly," Luther continued, "was the photographs. There were all these framed pictures...family photos of kids skiing, things like that. We just tore them off the walls and threw them across the room. It makes me sick thinking about it."

Alex asked softly, "What happened next?"

Luther shook his head and stared up at the ceiling of the hospital room. "We broke into another cabin. Fortunately, Warren found about six bottles of vodka and other stuff, so we went back to Troy's house.

"For days after that, I expected the police to come get us or something, but it never even got reported till a couple of weeks later. Once, I heard that the police had been asking around at school, but nothing ever came of it. I had

a feeling our coach knew but had smoothed it over somehow. It was like, because we were football players, we got
a free ride."

"Did anyone else on the team know about it?"

"Oh, yeah. As soon as we got back to the party, Warren
started bragging about it, and I told Chet the basics myself.
He said not to worry about it—that everyone does stuff
like that sometimes. We laughed it off, but over the next
few months I grew more and more angry with myself. It
just ate at me until I felt disgusted with the whole team,
and even with football."

"So that's when you quit?"

"No." Luther scratched at one of the bandages on his
arm. "The season was already over. I went out for
wrestling, but I didn't do very well. I think my feelings
about what had happened carried over into wrestling and
the whole sports, partying scene. By the time spring football practice rolled around, I just felt mad at everyone—
myself, Warren, the football coaches...the whole stupid
town—for making sports so important that it would drive
people to behave so...badly."

"So you decided not to go out."

Luther nodded. "Yeah, but even then, I didn't feel any
better. That didn't happen until I started working at Kay's.
At least I thought I was feeling better."

"You weren't?"

"I thought I was—until the fight with Warren."

"You mean it wasn't about Sal?"

Luther's eyes shifted back to Alex.

"Yeah, it was. Mostly. But it was also about that night after the last game. All along, I've been blaming Warren for what I did, and I took it out on him. In a way, it was his fault, but I could have done a lot of things differently."

Alex sat for a moment, looking at him. Then, she asked, "Why didn't you tell me all this before?"

Luther raised his eyes to hers. "I was ashamed. Hell, I never told anyone the whole story of what really happened and how I really felt about it. I...I guess I thought you wouldn't want to know me if you knew."

Alex shifted her gaze to the window. Luther wondered what she was thinking.

Finally she said, "You know, we're always taught there are good people and bad people, but I don't think that's true. I think we're all a mixture of all kinds of things, positive and negative. I think that good people sometimes make horrible mistakes and that rotten people can sometimes do really good things."

Luther's throat tightened.

"What I think is that you're basically a really wonderful person who made a mistake." Alex's blue eyes glistened. "It wasn't the worst mistake in the world, but I can tell you really feel bad about it. I just hope you can forgive yourself, so that you can keep doing all the amazing things you're doing now."

Alex's kind words unleashed a wave of pent-up emotion in Luther's chest.

"But," he said, his voice cracking, "how can you be so nice to me after the way I treated you when Sal got shot?"

Alex pursed her lips. "You *were* a jerk."

"I know. I'm sorry."

"But," Alex said, "I probably would have acted the same way."

They were again silent. Finally, Luther said, "Are we still friends?"

Alex stood up. "I'll have to think about it, but probably." As she said this, the dimple appeared in her cheek. Luther felt an urge to kiss her, and if his ribs hadn't hurt so much, he might even have tried. Instead, he asked, "Hey, how are the horses?"

"Except for the paint that died, they're great. They just cowered in the center of the pen and the fire didn't touch them. Brenda took good care of Diamond at your place."

"What happened to the rest of the town?"

"About a dozen people lost their homes, and that historic ranger station near the stables also burned. The helicopters and fire bombers from Missoula came in and dropped tons of fire retardant, and that stopped the flames at the edge of the east side. It still looks like a battle zone, though."

Luther tried to picture the scene in his mind. "I wish I could see it."

"Oh, you will."

Eighteen

The next day, he did.

Sunday morning, following one last check-up, the doctor discharged Luther from the hospital. His mom helped him to her car, and on the way home she gave him a quick tour. It was the first time Luther had seen a burn area so soon after a fire, and a lump formed in his stomach. Just outside of town, entire hillsides and fields had been reduced to charcoal and ash. The trunks of thousands of dead, blackened trees, some still smoldering, stood like jagged tombstones across the obliterated landscape.

In many places, Luther spotted the scorched remains of barns and other outbuildings, and the crumbling foundations of several houses that had been incinerated. The destruction was so complete, he could now see the river from everywhere along the old highway. Before, the view had always been obscured by trees and brush.

"God," he muttered as they drove.

"The Forest Service is saying most of this will start coming back as soon as we get the first rain," his mom said, "though the trees might take decades to grow back."

"Are they all dead?"

"A lot of them. Vic thinks some will recover. We won't know until next spring when the survivors start budding out again."

Luther nodded. Even though he knew that fire could be good for the ecosystem as a whole, the extent of the devastation hit him hard.

He didn't think it could get any worse until they reached the stables. His mom pulled into the deserted parking area and turned off the engine. The burned-out shell of Alex's dad's truck had been towed away, but the huge pile of charred beams and twisted metal from the barn still smoldered in front of them. When they rolled down the windows, the overpowering smell of smoke filled Luther's lungs. The stench triggered visions of the fire-engulfed structure crashing to the ground, launching flaming projectiles through the air.

"I can't believe someone set a fire like this on purpose," he said. "Whoever did this needs to pay."

His mom looked at him oddly. "Didn't Alex tell you?"

"Tell me what? Did they catch someone?"

"Oh, it's better than that. Your stepfather was the one who turned him in."

Luther's jaw dropped. "Vic? Vic caught the arsonist?"

His mother smiled. "Yep."

"Well, who was it?"

"A man named John Cristy. Ever heard of him?"

Luther shook his head. "There was a Ben Christy in wrestling last year. I wonder if it could have been his dad or his brother. Ben was really quiet, so I never talked to him much. Do they know *why* this guy was starting the fires?"

"The police haven't figured it all out, but radio reports said that Cristy works for Apple Mountain."

"Apple Mountain Timber?"

"Yes, and that's where it gets interesting. Rumor has it that Cristy's bosses at Apple Mountain actually encouraged him and a couple other guys—including Warren's brother Raymond—to go out there and set some of these fires."

Luther shifted in his seat, trying to get more comfortable. The binding around his rib cage made it impossible. "Why in the world would Apple Mountain want to start fires?" he asked.

"That's what we all wondered at first. But apparently Apple Mountain was counting on the fires to open up public lands to salvage logging. All of the fires Cristy set were on National Forest and Montana state lands, in areas that had been closed to logging. Apple Mountain figured that the public would consider it a waste of good wood to leave dead trees just standing there and demand that the timber companies cut them down. That's happened in the past, and I guess Apple Mountain figured it would go that way again."

"And, of course, Apple Mountain would get the wood," Luther said.

"Exactly. According to an article in today's *Missoulian,* it was an attempt to make an end-run around logging restrictions."

"That is so twisted," Luther exclaimed. "Don't they realize that a lot of their own land burned up as a result of the fires?"

"Apparently the company didn't mind that so much," his mother said. "Apple Mountain had already completely logged the big trees in those areas and was planning to sell the land for vacation homes and subdevelopments. Burning off those lands might even make them easier to develop or sell."

"Did Cristy set the Demming fire?"

"They think so—maybe with help from Raymond Juddson and some others."

"Well, that would explain how Raymond's kept his job at the mill."

"And perhaps why Warren and his dad have been raising so much of a ruckus. If they knew what Raymond was up to, they'd want to distract people from what was actually going on."

Or maybe Warren just wanted to prove he could be as big a jerk as his brother, Luther thought. A lot of things were starting to make sense. "So how did Vic catch them?" he asked.

"Vic told me he and Clifton Hanks saw this Cristy fellow driving by with a couple of gas cans in the back of his truck. Vic said he got a feeling that something just wasn't right about it, so on a hunch, he and Clifton began following him around and spied him checking out a spot. They told the police, and when Cristy went back out there, Federal agents were waiting for him."

"Has he confessed?"

His mom started the car and eased it into drive. "Everyone around town thinks he'll cut a deal—which is bad news for Apple Mountain if they really are involved."

Luther was speechless as his mom pulled out of the stables parking lot and back onto the road. When they'd almost reached their house, his mom said, "Oh, I forgot to tell you. Kay came by earlier. She said to tell you to come out when you're ready. She's got a lot of work for you to do."

Luther looked at her. "She's not still mad at me?"

His mother shrugged. "You'll have to ask her yourself."

That night, Luther ate an early dinner with his mother and sister. By then, his ribs and arm were throbbing again, so he popped one of the codeine pills the doctor had prescribed and went to his room to lie down. About nine o'clock, he heard Vic's truck drive up and, a few minutes later, a knock on the door.

"Yeah?" Luther called.

The door swung open and Vic said, "Mind if I come in?"

Luther shook his head and raised himself into a sitting position. Vic still wore his soot-covered firefighting clothes and held his helmet in his hands. He sat at the foot of the bed. "How's the arm and ribs?"

"They hurt."

Vic grunted. "I'm not surprised after the heroics you pulled. That was pretty impressive. You're lucky you didn't get hurt worse."

Luther was startled to hear him say something so, well, positive.

They sat awkwardly for a moment. Luther watched a small spider scurry across the ceiling. Then, Vic said, "Look Luther, I'm not really good at this fatherhood thing. I'm sure you've figured that out by now."

Luther cracked a fleeting smile.

"It's never easy having stepkids," Vic continued, running his hand through his thinning hair. "Just like I'm sure it's not easy having a stepparent. But even with Brenda... shoot, the whole parent-kid thing is a pain in the ass a lot of the time. At least, I remember it was with me and my old man."

Luther just listened. He'd never heard his stepfather say much of anything about his own childhood before.

"This probably won't be the last of our scrapes," Vic went on, shifting his eyes to the door. "I can be an idiot sometimes, and you don't always make it easy yourself. This whole forest thing you're doing...I don't get it. But what I'm trying to say is...I guess you're old enough to do what you've got to do. Me, I'll try to be more patient about things—even if I don't agree with them. That sound fair?"

"Okay," Luther said.

"Okay." Vic stood and started for the door.

"Vic?"

His stepfather turned toward him.

Luther wasn't sure how to begin. "It's about the fires. I'm really proud of what you did, turning those guys in."

Vic nodded, his mouth a straight line.

"But I have to tell you that for a while, I thought—"

Vic held up his hand and stopped him. "Whatever it was, Luther, I don't need to know. We all think up some crazy stuff sometimes. Me too. I haven't given you nearly the credit you deserve lately. Let's just leave it at that and both try to do a little better."

After Chet got out of school on Wednesday, he came by to pick up Luther. They drove to the police station and parked.

Still sitting in the car, Chet said, "You sure you want to do this, Luth?"

Luther took a deep breath—as deep as his broken ribs would allow. "Yeah. You still in?"

"If that's what you want."

"Thanks. I appreciate it."

They walked into the station, and Luther asked to see the sergeant on duty. A receptionist showed them to the right office, and the sergeant invited them to sit down.

"What can I do for you fellas?" the officer asked, his face etched with fatigue from the past few days.

Luther exchanged a last look with Chet. Then, he told the sergeant all about the party and the house break-ins the year before. Surprise replaced fatigue on the officer's face, and he picked up a pen and began taking notes, interrupting now and then to ask a question or clarify a detail. He also asked Chet to confirm what Luther was saying. It took about twenty minutes.

When he had finally finished telling his story, Luther asked, "So what now?" His heart pounded as he waited for an answer.

The sergeant tapped his pen on the desk for a moment and stared down at his notes.

"Well, Luther, it's like this," he finally said. "With this fire, we're swamped. We've got better things to do than lock you up, and with your appetite, we probably couldn't afford to feed you anyway. Also, after what you did during the fire, I don't know how Heartwood citizens would take to having one of their local heroes thrown in the slammer."

Luther managed a smile.

"Let me ask you," the sergeant said. "Do you understand that it was wrong what you did? I mean, all of it. Not just breaking into the house, but the drinking, too?"

Luther looked the sergeant straight in the eyes. "Yes."

The sergeant returned his stare. "I believe you," he said, nodding. "Are you willing to pay back your part of the damage you caused?"

"Yes."

"You have a job?"

"I'm...not sure. But I'll get one if I have to."

"Okay. Then, let's keep this informal. I'll put you in touch with the owners of the homes. They live over in Helena, and I'll tell them I've talked to you. You write them a formal letter of apology and, together with them, figure out a repayment schedule. That way, I don't have to clog up the city docket with this case."

"What about Warren and Chris Martin?" Chet asked.

The sergeant set down his pen. "I know Chris's family. I'll work out something similar with them. Warren, well, this is the least of his family's troubles. I might have to get a little more what you'd call 'hands-on' with his case."

The sergeant stood up, and Chet and Luther followed his lead. The officer said, "As long as you adhere to your part of the bargain, I consider this matter resolved."

"Thank you."

The sergeant stood and shook hands with both boys. "You did the right thing coming in."

Nineteen

espite his mom's protests, Luther hobbled back to school on Thursday, as soon as his suspension ended. He was greeted by a frenzy of activity. Camera crews from the national networks swarmed the perimeter of the school grounds, interviewing kids and reporting on the fire aftermath. Overhead, National Guard helicopters carried politicians on a tour of the burn area. Montana's governor, along with the U.S. Secretary of the Interior, flew over to observe the damage.

Luther attracted his own share of attention. Dozens of kids asked him about the fires at the stables and at Kay's place. A reporter from *The Missoulian* got permission to interview him between classes and bombarded him with questions. By noon, Luther had had enough. To escape the hoopla, he took his lunch out to the bleachers. A few minutes later, Alex showed up. "I thought I might find you here. Is this any place for a bona fide hero to eat?"

Luther was pleased Alex had found him. "How's it going?"

"Pretty well. I really should be getting ready for our SFS meeting tomorrow."

"You're still going to meet?" Luther asked.

"We're still going to meet. You wouldn't believe how many kids have asked about it since everything came out about the fires. There's a real interest in learning more and thinking up projects to help the forest recover."

"I never expected that."

"Plant a small seed and big things can grow—just like I told you."

"Well, you told me *something,* anyway," Luther replied, already wondering what the group could do with more members.

"I've got some bad news, though," Alex said. "I talked to my dad about Sal."

Luther's chest tightened. "Have they been able to prove Warren did it?"

Alex shook her head. "It doesn't look like they will, either."

"What about the people he told?"

"My dad interviewed them, but no one told him anything he could use in a case."

"But Chet overheard Warren—"

"It's too sketchy. There's just no real evidence he did it," Alex said. "I'm sorry."

Luther hadn't really expected they'd be able to nail Warren, but disappointment still hit him. He stared down at his feet.

"I know you think it was your fault, Luther, but it wasn't.

You didn't shoot Sal. And if it's any consolation," Alex added, "most people have turned on Warren. Everyone knows what he did, and people are barely talking to him. In a lot of ways, he's getting punished for the shooting."

Luther didn't say anything for a moment. Then he said, "You want to hear something weird? Sitting in the hospital, I thought a lot about Warren. At first, I wanted to kill him."

"You sure *tried*."

A smile flickered across Luther's lips, but he again grew serious. "Yeah, but now, I don't anymore. Since I heard about his brother Raymond being involved in the fires and maybe his dad, too, I've just been thinking that if I'd been born into that family, I'd probably be as screwed up as Warren is. Even though Knot Juddson is a jerk, he's still Warren's dad, and Warren probably wants Knot to be proud of him—even if it's for doing stupid things. You know what I mean?"

Alex hooked a strand of her reddish hair over her right ear. "I think so."

"The thing is, my real dad was almost that bad. I keep wondering how I would have ended up if my mom hadn't gotten away from him. Maybe I would have been just like Warren."

"I doubt *that*."

Luther shrugged. "But you don't ever know, do you? Even though I want Warren to be held responsible for what he did, I saw him today and realized that I mostly just wish..."

"What?" Alex asked.

"I just wish none of this had ever happened."

The following Monday, Luther came home from school and changed into his bird clothes. Roadkill in tow, he pedaled his sister's bike one-handed to Kay's. Luther couldn't believe how desolate the farm looked. The house stood like a lonely survivor amid a black desert of ash and charred wood. Luther found Kay sitting on the stump of the fallen ponderosa pine, scribbling notes on a pad of paper.

Roadkill ran ahead of Luther and pulled Kay from her concentration. When she looked up, her mouth spread into a smile. "Hey Luth, how's my favorite face?"

"Better. Thanks." As he approached, he noticed Kay had set up temporary birdcages in Max's pen. He saw Max walking around but didn't see the bald eagle.

"Where's Groucho?" Luther asked.

"Aw, he was ready, so I sent him on his way," Kay said. "I had enough to keep track of and had to make room. You wouldn't believe how many new birds have poured in since the fire. So, how are the ribs?"

Luther waved his hand. "They're okay. They still hurt, but it's nothing too bad."

"I'm not sure whether to thank you for saving the place or bawl you out for taking so many chances. I still can't believe you jumped off the roof! What made you do that?"

Luther had asked himself the same question a dozen times. "I don't know. It was the fastest way down?"

Kay laughed. "Yeah, sure. Whatever. Just don't do it *again*."

"I'll try not to," he said with a grin. "What're you doing, anyway?"

"Well, I decided to look at the fire as an opportunity," Kay told him. "Instead of just jury-rigging old sheds like we did before, I thought I'd build us some proper bird-houses with heating, good lighting, the whole works— maybe even go for Jacuzzis and satellite TV."

"Sounds expensive."

"Yeah, but I've been getting a ton of donations to put things back together. A couple of the local stations did news spots on what happened, and the story was picked up nationally. The money's been pouring in."

"That's great."

"Yeah, in Heartwood. Can you believe it? I think I've got at least enough in the bank for two houses with room to hold eight birds apiece. Maybe even more."

"Who's going to build them?"

Kay looked at him. "When can you start?"

❧

Luther didn't build the birdhouses alone. A local contractor named Jake Lonski volunteered his crew to dig and pour the foundations, do the basic framing, and run plumbing and wiring. With that done, Luther set to work after school and on weekends installing windows, putting on fireproof roofs, and building the birdcages inside the buildings. Vic joined him half a dozen times to help with tricky parts, and Alex pitched in when she wasn't helping put things back together at the stables.

By the time Luther finished installing the insulation, the weather had cooled considerably. Two fall storms had dumped several inches of rain, and within days green shoots had turned the burn areas into dazzling emerald carpets. Though the surviving trees wouldn't bud out until spring, all kinds of bunch grasses and other native plants started poking up through the black duff. Robins, meadowlarks, woodpeckers, flickers, and other birds appeared in droves to fatten up on exposed seeds, insects, and other delicacies.

When he wasn't at Kay's, Luther saw Alex as much as possible. As co-presidents of SFS, they held lunchtime meetings once a week with the new members and planned activities to help the burn areas recover. Along streamsides and other sensitive areas they helped Forest Service teams plant grasses, willows, and other native plants to control runoff and erosion. They also helped install physical barriers to slow water as it flowed down steep hillsides. Unfortunately, the seeds of knapweed, leafy spurge, Canada thistle, and dozens of other noxious weeds quickly sprouted from some of the burn areas. To keep them from driving out native wildflowers and grasses, the SFS organized work parties to pull the invaders.

One Saturday in early November, Luther asked Brenda to drop him off at Kay's. He wanted to finish off the cages in Hawk Heaven II before the really cold weather screamed down from the arctic.

"That can wait," Kay told him when he got there. "Come here. I want to show you something."

Luther and Roadkill followed Kay into her house, and they entered the tiny living room. Luther saw a cardboard box sitting on the coffee table.

"What's that?" he asked, remembering the mangled bird they'd had to euthanize earlier in the fall.

Kay gave him a conspiratorial look. "Open it."

Luther carefully pulled up the lid. Inside, on a heating pad, sat a male red-tail hawk.

"Watch out," Kay warned him. "He might try to get out."

"He's beautiful," Luther said.

"Isn't he? He's got a good weight, too."

"Where'd you get him?"

"A local rancher saw him go after a jackrabbit. He came in so fast that he missed the rabbit and cold-cocked himself against a tree stump."

"Is he all right?"

"He might have a slight concussion—not to mention a headache—but he'll be 100 percent in a couple of days."

"That's great," said Luther. "We'll be able to let him go again."

"Actually, I thought we might hang onto him for a while."

"Keep him? Why?"

"Gee," Kay said in a sarcastic voice, "I thought someone around here wanted to be a falconer."

The light bulb finally clicked on in Luther's head. "Really? I can have him?"

"I think he'd be perfect," Kay said. "He's under a year old, the ideal age to train a bird. Once you get his hunting skills up, we'll let him go and he'll have a much better chance to survive. Then, maybe we'll get you a falcon.

"I mean, if you still want to," Kay added with a smile.

"Hell yes, I want to!"

From then on Luther spent every spare moment at Kay's. Over Alex's objections, Luther had named the red-tail "Rabbitslayer" because of the way he'd knocked himself out. After feeding the other birds, Luther and Kay took out the hawk and went through the gradual process of training him. Luther got him used to stepping onto his hand and rewarded him with food each time he cooperated. Within days, he had the hawk—tethered to a line—flying from a post to his hand.

In late November, after almost a month of training, the Chinooks blew warm from the south and west. Temperatures rose to the high forties, and Kay told Luther it was time for Rabbitslayer to take his first big test.

"Are you sure he's ready?" Luther asked.

"You're never sure what'll happen the first time," Kay told him. "But you've done great work with him. It's time to find out what this baby can do."

The next afternoon, the day before Thanksgiving, Alex

picked up Luther and Roadkill and drove them down to Kay's. Kay was waiting with her camera.

"I want to photodocument this," she said.

Luther felt like someone was dribbling basketballs in his stomach.

"Go get Rabbitslayer, and I'll meet you out in the field," Kay told him.

Luther and Alex walked to Hawk Heaven II and stepped inside.

"Talk about deluxe accommodations," Alex said as Luther walked over to the new cage that held Rabbitslayer. "You nervous?"

Luther's hand shook as he put on the glove. "I don't think I've been this scared since last year's district wrestling championship."

"Did you win?" Alex asked.

"No."

"You will this time," she said. "And maybe this will help."

Alex spun Luther around, placed her arms around his neck, and pressed her lips to his. It took Luther a moment to realize what was happening. Then, he kissed her back. The wet warmth from her mouth spread through every nerve in his body, and he forgot all about the red-tail.

Finally, Alex pulled away. "Easy boy. You've got work to do."

"It can wait," Luther said, leaning toward her again.

Alex laughed and pressed her hand to his chest. "Later. I promise."

His heart still thundering—whether from the kiss or the coming flight, he couldn't tell—Luther took Rabbitslayer from his cage, placed the radio transmitters on his jesses, and, with Alex beside him, carried the hawk out to the field.

"What took you so long?" Kay asked, but the smirk on her face showed she had a pretty good idea. "You all ready?"

"As ready as I'm going to be," Luther answered. He took out a small piece of quail and fed it to Rabbitslayer— one last reminder to the bird that coming back meant getting fed. Alex called Roadkill and crouched down with the dog about forty feet away to make sure he didn't do anything to upset the hawk.

"Okay," said Kay, her camera at the ready. "Let him rip."

Luther took a deep breath, swung his hand up and released Rabbitslayer's jesses.

The red-tail launched himself skyward. His take-off wasn't as effortless as Sal's—red-tails were built for soaring, not quick acceleration—but flapping hard, the hawk gained altitude and then circled to the east. Luther held his breath as the bird banked left.

The hawk made a wide arc and soared past him toward the river. Luther's heart rate again picked up. "Uh-oh," he said to himself. "He's out of here."

But instead of flying away, the bird angled left and headed toward Sal's old snag. Even though its trunk had been charred, the snag had somehow survived the fire and still stood near the river. As Luther, Kay, and Alex watched, Rabbitslayer alighted on Sal's favorite perch.

Mouths open, Luther and Kay stared at each other.

"What are the chances of that?" Kay said, and Luther saw tears form in her eyes.

Then Kay raised the camera viewfinder. "Okay, Luth. Call him."

Luther pulled out a piece of quail, placed it between his thumb and forefinger, and held his hand up to where the red-tail could easily see it. "Hup!" he shouted.

The red-tail looked at him, then twisted his head to look downstream. Luther tried to stay calm.

"Come on, Rabbit!" he said, and yelled "Hup!" once more.

The hawk looked back at him, and after a quick glance to his right, leaped off the perch. He swooped down low to the ground, flapped four times in a straight line, and then rose to Luther's clenched fist.

"Good bird," Luther said. He firmly grasped the bird's jesses between his fingers, and the red-tail tore at the meat in his gloved hand. Alex clapped softly behind him.

Kay, who'd been firing a string of pictures of the flight, shouted, "Perfect!"

Acknowledgments

I never could have written this book without extensive input from a number of people. First and foremost, I'd like to offer a soaring thank-you to Kate Davis, Director of Raptors of the Rockies, a nonprofit group dedicated to education about birds of prey. Kate not only provided vital information about her operations for this book, but was generous enough to read over and comment on the manuscript. Her husband Tom was also very generous with his time. I urge readers to take a look at Kate's website, *www.raptorsoftherockies.org.*

I'd also like to thank Dave Strohmaier, a fire expert and author of the excellent book *Drift Smoke,* for reviewing the manuscript and offering guidance on the discussion of fires and forest policy. A galloping thank-you to my writer's group for their suggestions, especially Wendy and Ray Norgaard for correcting my many misconceptions about horses. Thanks, too, to Jim Chaffin and his gyrfalcon Chantilly Lace for allowing me to witness the awesome spectacle of falconry first-hand; Mike Paterni, Budget Officer for the United States Forest Service for giving me insights into the Bitterroot fires of 2000; Wendel Hann, National Fire Ecologist for the U.S.F.S., for his perspective on fire supression, timber management, and forest ecology;

George Weldon, U.S.F.S. Deputy Directory of Fire Aviation and Air for information on fire recovery; and Joe Jaquith of the Montana Department of Fish, Wildlife, and Parks for providing me with details of falconry regulations.

Additional thanks go to Michael Parrish for keeping me up-to-date on high school activism; James Corbin and my main man Dr. Eric Dawson for teaching me all about boxer's fractures and other "combat injuries"; Paul Moe for telling me about small-town Montana football; Barb and Ron Scherry of Great Northern Books for their Billings perspective; and Erica Wirtala for additional "horse help" and for spotting the greatest Border collie who ever lived.

Finally, I'd like to thank the many talented people at Peachtree who worked together to make this book soar, especially my gifted editor Vicky Holifield. Thank you for your endless patience and for always thinking of better ideas.

S. B. C. III

About the Author

SNEED B. COLLARD III is a biologist, world traveler, speaker, and author of more than fifty award-winning books for young people, including THE PRAIRIE BUILDERS, ONE NIGHT IN THE CORAL SEA, and SHEP: OUR MOST LOYAL DOG. His first novel, DOG SENSE, has collected many honors, including the 2005 ASPCA Henry Bergh Award. Sneed was also named *The Washington Post*–Children's Book Guild 2006 Nonfiction Children's Writer of the Year. To learn more about Sneed, explore his website, *www.sneedbcollardiii.com*.